Goya, Are You With Me Now?

Books by H. E. Francis

THE SUDDEN TREES AND OTHER STORIES

A DISTURBANCE OF GULLS

NAMING THINGS

HAD

THE HISTORY OF A MAN IN DESPAIR

THE ITINERARY OF BEGGARS

Goya, Are You With Me Now?

H. E. Francis

Frederic C. Beil
Savannah

Copyright © 1999 by H. E. Francis

First published in the United States by
Frederic C. Beil, Publisher, Inc.
609 Whitaker Street
Savannah, Georgia 31401
http://www.beil.com

LIBRARY OF CONGRESS CATALOGING-IN-PUBLICATION DATA
Francis, H. E. (Herbert Edward), 1924–
Goya, are you with me now? / by H. E. Francis
p.   cm.
ISBN 1-929490-01-1 (alk. paper)
I. Title
PS3556.R328G69   2000   99-39523
813'.54—dc21   CIP

This book is set in Galliard, composed by SkidType,
Savannah, Georgia; printed on acid-free paper; and sewn in signatures.

Printed in the United States of America

To
Virginia

As I see it,
painting and religious experience are the same thing,
and what we are all searching for is
the understanding and realization of infinity.

Ben Nicholson

Goya, Are You With Me Now?

It was not Esther who called, as I might have expected, though she and Brand had been divorced for years, not his mother, but his grandfather—from Bristol. That was fitting because only his grandparents really knew how close Brand and I had been and for how long. His grandfather sounded close, as if he were here in Madrid. I could hear his grandmother's voice too, bolstering his grandfather perhaps, because his voice quavered—it seldom did.

"Brand is dead," he said.

"Brand!" It came as a whisper.

"*Paul*," I heard her say. He was *Brand* to me.

"Paul," his grandfather said.

"Paul," I said—too loud now.

It was not to his grandfather, but to Brand I cried it out. I thought—I knew I was thinking—*Brand, you have no right to do this to me*, though I was thinking too it wasn't possible, I'd been with him just a couple of weeks ago, he'd been resting since his collapse not long after the boy's execution in Alabama, at Atmore. He'd been improving. We had talked and talked.

Of course I must have said all that to his grandfather, who knew all that too but who, like me, in that strange but normal way, would be consoled by talk of him, talk of any kind rather than hang up and cut it off, end it.

When I hung up I didn't immediately remember all he'd said because we had gone on talking fumblingly, the way you sometimes do at such moments unless you both know the facts beforehand, your mind even against your will repeating what has been said. But after, I did remember that—that I had thought, I had uttered silently to myself, *Brand, you have no right to do this to me.* It was not the fact of his death—his grandfather had said clearly "Brand is dead"—but the other fact that goaded, when he had gone on a bit, when perhaps he had screwed up his courage to say what he would surely not say to everyone, there would be no need, most relatives would surely try to conceal the fact from outsiders.

"By his own hand," his grandfather had said.

What remained after our conversation—it was long—were those few hard words:

Brand is dead.

By his own hand.

Stone the words might have been. Isolated. In the air.

But what I saw in the air was the bridge, the Mount Hope bridge in Bristol, as if it really stood there spanning the sky over Madrid.

I closed my eyes. Madrid vanished, but the bridge remained, and I saw the bay, sky painfully blue, the edging clouds, the green ferry stark, the green islands, and left that long stretch of Tiverton coast across the bay, stark too, painfully beautiful.

And Brand and me sitting on the stone wall under the bridge on the tip of town called The Ferry, after the landing which boats crossed to regularly before the bridge had been built.

Brand's first photographs were of the bridge in fog. The blurred cables and girders suggested a great web concealed under fog. From the first day that he saw the bridge as a boy new in town, he was obsessed by it.

"Why don't you ever photograph the bridge on clear days?" I once asked him.

"Because then it's just a bridge between Bristol and Portsmouth."

His answer was that laugh, guttural, but he was serious. He had a kind of Germanic heaviness that I came to associate with the Nordic world his parents had come from.

On clear days the Mount Hope bridge is a long arch over the bay, its beauty and grace enough to make you proud that men can conceive and execute such perfection.

"What else would it be?"

"An image."

"Of what?"

He laughed. "You can't say. That's what an image is. Ask Miss Bradford. 'Is this a dagger which I see before me?'"

We laughed. She was English lit. Staid, dull, laughable sometimes, but solid.

"You mean it says it for you."

"I mean it makes you see what's really there."

In class Miss Bradford had said, "The dagger conjures up the invisible landscape that is always there waiting. Macbeth *sees* its horrors."

"Words are better," I said.

"Why?"

"Because anybody can make his own picture out of the word, but he has to take your photo of the bridge as it is, he can't change it."

He thought a bit.

"But that doesn't keep you from seeing what I see."

"No. But it's not what I might see."

"Good thing!"

He laughed.

He said, "I have lots of images."

"Maybe you'll have to put them all together someday."

He went serious. "I intend to."

For Brand images were alive. Not until he had become obsessed with photography did he articulate about images—photography would become his field. He *felt* images profoundly. The same look could come over his face that came over the faces of some of the old Portuguese women at St. Elizabeth's or the Italians at Our Lady of Mount Carmel when the Virgin or Jesus was carried past to wafts of rich incense in the holy day processions and stared stunned or lowered their eyes at what was beautiful and unbearable. I was fascinated by the ritual, but I always tried to hold my breath until the incense was dissipated, not to contaminate my Protestant soul.

For us tenth grade students, Brand himself was an image. On the first day of classes there he sat, the only unknown, tall and thin with rich blond hair and light blue eyes, his face badly broken out—perhaps why he was sitting quite rigid and looking straight ahead, though if he were trying to be inconspicuous, he achieved the opposite effect. When he did turn to you, he had an innocent look, his alert eyes filled with curiosity or wonder, and he could smile or laugh with the spontaneity of a flash of light.

Miss Bradford called the roll.

"Paul Brand."

All heads turned. We had been waiting for his name.

"Brand here."

If that "Brand here" for an instant made me think *foreign*, *military*, his faultless English quickly dispelled my suspicion, though not long after I would realize that such impeccable English in a fifteen-year-old was suspect too, enough to make you wonder.

The first week he signed up for the Photography Club. We actually talked for the first time in the darkroom, setting it up—lights, wires and clips, trays, developers.

"The solution has to be exact," he said.

"Yes. Perfect."

He laughed. He had hit the right note. He was precision personified. He didn't say much. I liked that. It was a good sign.

From the time he moved to town to live with his grandparents, he had a reputation for silence. One of our bonds from the beginning was the pleasure of long silences without the discomfort that silences cause most people, though like me he could talk a blue streak with anybody who struck on one of his interests. People took his silences for shyness. Sometimes—when his skin broke out badly, for example—he *was* self-conscious; he would stare through people as if no one were there to see his face. But he would burst out of a stillness with a spontaneous smile and a strange question that could jar our little mental universe into motion: "But suppose all of us refused to go to church?" "Burn all our books and then what would happen?"

4

"If schools closed, how much could our parents teach us?"

His parents he hardly ever mentioned, but he loved his grandparents. They lived in a two-story house on Wood Street, which led straight to the cove and, a long mile after, to The Ferry. My own street, Hope, which ran parallel to it, followed the waterfront and at the edge of town curved into Wood. It was a long time before he would invite me in—old world customs, maybe—but it was obvious he loved the house and town.

"My grandparents—on my mother's side—came over not long after my parents were settled in Alabama, but they wanted a climate more like their own. Most immigrants do."

"And didn't your parents?"

"My father had no choice. He was brought over to work for the government."

Like many Germans his grandparents loved fine music, and it was a pleasure, especially in warm weather when all the windows were open, to sit on his front porch and hear his grandmother play the piano. Brand himself played—he'd taken formal lessons—and during the periods when his nerves bothered him and his skin broke out, less frequently the longer he lived in town, he clung closer to home and consoled himself with playing. Otherwise, he read photography or worked in a darkroom he had set up in his cellar or hiked hours in the woods and over the peninsula. His grandparents let him explore his own world; they never insisted, he said, on pushing him into their choices.

It was a long time before his grandparents asked me into the house. Usually I would wait out back or sit on the front porch steps till Brand came out, though with his punctuality he seldom kept me waiting. He rarely talked about them—or his parents. They must have been very withdrawn, as so many Germans were, knowing how my parents' generation felt about them because of the Hitler war. So I was startled when his grandfather met me at the door one day after school and said, "Come in, Ferris. It's good to know you. We are slow with the courtesies. I must apologize."

I smiled at "apologize."

5

His grandmother said, "Oh, you're as familiar to us as the mailman!" and laughed warmly. "We're just having tea. I've just made some *Lebkuchen.*"

Both spoke good English though with heavy accents. If I knew next to nothing about them, they knew all about me. At home Brand must have been a talker and very open with them. They must have felt I was family because we sat, very much at home, in the kitchen. I could see in the room beyond the dining room a wall of books. One of the few facts Brand had mentioned was that his grandfather had been a partner in a prosperous publishing house, his wife a teacher in the *gymnasium.* They were both tall and attractive, older versions of Brand— you could see their common descent when they stood together —and as gentle as Brand himself. He could have been their son. After that, I never had to wait outside.

It was hard not to ask questions about his parents, and though Brand was always as obliging as he could be, it was clear he didn't want to cast shadows over his family or mislead me. Mostly I had wondered why they didn't visit him.

"Because I have to spend summers with them."

"Why do you have to?"

"Because I promised them I would."

"Why'd you have to promise them that?"

"So they'd let me go!"

His laughter cut off my questioning. I was sensitive enough not to ask after that.

From that first year there is a photo of my fox terrier, Tommy, sitting in the wooden armchair at my desk like a canine Henry James, a forepaw poised as if to write on the air for all eternity. That spring I entered Tommy in the annual Club contest. Brand agonized over which photo of the bridge to submit. Even at that stage he knew more about technique than I have ever learned. What he did enter was by any standard masterful. I was certain he would win first—he should have won it—but the blue ribbon went to "Tommy." Brand's bridge won the gold. I dreaded to see Brand—I was hurt for him, I was sorry I'd entered, it was awkward that I'd won. What the judges didn't see was the enormous talent revealed in Brand's photo. But Brand! You'd have thought *he'd* won. "Tommy!" He seized the ribbon and danced it through the air, laughing in a kind of frenzy, an orgy. It was a release I'd never known in him. He was terribly alive, all light. It was then I came to suspect the enormity of the affection behind that quiet facade, for he was absolutely selfless at that moment. In a sense he *had* won, because he so identified with me. He already had that genius— perhaps, I thought at the time, that was his only genius?—for so identifying with the other that he virtually became the other. And as if I knew that—I didn't—when he stopped and stood there, so happy for me, I said, "I want you to have 'Tommy' and the ribbon." "Me!" Caught off guard, he was as suddenly deeply serious. I could have sworn his eyes filled, but in an instant he was smiling again. "Mine. 'Tommy.'"

Like his height and his blond hair and blue eyes, his voice, the heavy tones, struck me as Nordic too, perhaps because for me he came to embody everything his father's generation wanted to preserve exclusively.

Dead.

By his own hand.

He was never so alive as on days when we would walk from town to The Ferry and sit under the bridge and watch the ferry come and go and sometimes at night identify the stars.

At night The Ferry, together with the long private roads down to the homes on the harbor, was a parking place for lovers, but by day people went for the view of Portsmouth and Island Park and across the bay Tiverton. Many of the boys liked to hang around for the pleasure of surprising couples "in the act," but I was satisfied with a few clues to let my imagination elaborate my own version of sex, and Brand idealized women. That would be, in the most passionate affair of his life (it was), a major obstacle in his marriage to Esther and in his happiness with other women.

I think in his sexual moments there was always some confusion in his mind between the women in his life and his mother. That first summer he both desired and feared going back to his family in Alabama. It must have been that confusion that made him, as June approached, twitchy about everything and then nervous in some deeply organic way because his face broke out badly. It shamed him. No medication would help. I saw how preoccupied his grandparents were, but of course they were helpless—his parents had their conditions and he had promised and all of them would observe the promise.

For me the first summer was a disaster of lonely wandering. He had become my right arm. One consolation, and theirs too they told me, was that I went to his grandparents' house all summer long as if he were there. "It's like having Paul with us." The other consolation was his letters. Perhaps because he felt so alone and nostalgic and could talk out his always reserved—repressed—side and because he had known me, his only close friend, long enough now, in bits here and there he let himself go. I think now he did it intentionally, he wanted me to know, and he could write what might be too hard for him to say face to face. But it was also, I believe, a deliberate act of trust—he was telling me what I was to him, he wanted to be sure I knew.

My grandparents, Brand wrote, *said my mother was always hypersensitive, but before she came to the U.S. it had reached the proportions of a disease.* Organic, *the doctors said. She'll never get over it. They thought she'd lose me.*

He wrote, *Though my mother wants me always with her, when I'm in Bristol she feels I've been sent to a safe place where nothing can threaten me. I had to argue and argue to convince them to let me live in Bristol. I was getting so nervous. They were afraid I'd end up like my mother.*

He wrote, *At the end of the war, when my mother found out she was pregnant, she almost went out of her mind because she was afraid of so many things.*

When Brand came back in the fall, he was nervous, not well, and at first he stayed home a good bit of the time—it was his face again—and I often studied with him there. He had an enormous

8

rear room on the second floor with bookcases and cubbyholes and a walk-in closet big enough for a darkroom, though he had set up his workplace in a small room in the rear right half of the cellar, walled off from the coal bin and furnace and the other half with his Ping-Pong table and his grandmother's winter clothesline.

For a while we lived like moles come out only for classes. Then something happened to all of us—to me and Brand and the whole class. A new girl had come to town. She had come as much out of nowhere as Brand had and aroused as much interest—at first because she was very tall and beautiful, blond with creamy complexion and glowing as if she carried sun; but then because she was simply good, kind, and attentive to everyone, and as natural as family, all of which of course made her absolutely unusual. Nobody could believe Clara Harmon hadn't descended from a cloud to give us mortals a glimpse of the angelic spheres.

Everybody fell for Clara—boys, girls, teachers—yet she went through the days without an iota of self-consciousness and seemed to satisfy everyone while she was at school though she lived a rather restricted social life after classes. She lived on The Neck, the narrow stretch of land between Bristol and Warren, so always she came and went on the bus or in a family car with Bett Wilkinson and Emily Prince and Emily's brother Bill and now and again others who lived not far from her. Theirs was a kind of snob circle without the condescension of snobbism, an aura reinforced when one of the rich Herreshoff girls decided to attend the high school instead of a private school.

Brand broke the circle. He went for Bett with her cropped hair, her long lithe outdoor Ingrid Bergman freshness, Bett the athlete, who would walk the several miles to town with Emily Prince on Saturdays to hike with us because Brand "could talk the shirt off anyone in the school" and "between the two, Brand and Ferris, you weren't bored for a minute." So we became—Brand and Bett and Emily and I—a constant foursome. The girls spent more and more time weekdays in town, and nights we took long walks together. After, Brand and I would walk back to town, then, reluctant to go in, walk each other home—during our senior year sometimes half the night back and forth between each other's house—until one night Brand, who had been holding back his secret for some time, said he had to tell me it wasn't Bett but Emily—he'd fallen for Emily.

"I can't help it," he said, "honest, Ferris."

In the moonlight I could see tears in his eyes.

"You don't hate me, do you?"

It was our first—our only—rift. It left me silent.

He gripped me by the shoulders.

"You don't, do you?"

He was so torn. I felt the initial betrayal. All my loyalties were challenged. I thought he needn't have told me, he could have gone on suffering in silence, but that wouldn't have been fair to any of us, least of all to Bett. But Brand had his sense of honor, of idealism; he couldn't live the lie. And he had made Emily perfectly aware of his feelings, and she had made tantamount to a rejection. He was too serious for her; she'd have nothing like that in mind for a long time, she said. It broke the circle: Bett knew, Emily knew. Soon the seriousness of our relationships must have reached their parents because too abruptly we were cut off except for school hours and extracurricular activities.

But behind it all was Clara. Brand had done a series of photos of Clara. She was classically beautiful and the photos were awesome. It took me a while to realize that what Brand really worshiped—what he called love, at first in Bett and then in Emily—was a reflection of an image of beauty and harmony, an ideal, perhaps the only thing all his life long that would never tarnish. It was something he refused to—or couldn't—give up. It was something he insisted on believing in. But he was denied it. It had rejected him. And then it was beyond his reach. It became a tragedy for all of us—at the very end of our senior year, Clara Harmon died of leukemia. None of us knew until almost graduation what it was she had been suffering from, which had taken her so rapidly. It was the saddest of graduations. For Brand—

and only I could know it—a living image of the unreachable ideal had gone out of the world. "How lucky," he would say long after, "that I took all those photos of Clara Harmon." He still had his image—and he believed in it—though he did not yet know how far removed from him the actual image was. But it was the face he would go searching for, years. It would come to be something inviolable that he refused to believe did not exist. He would go looking for proof of its existence, and it would be years before he found the face, and it would be only in the worst situation, as it had been each time he had had an inkling of that ideal, which he would find devastatingly inseparable from the real through which he had glimpsed it.

Brand was the salutatorian at graduation. When it was announced, we celebrated at my house. Brand loved my mother, envied me the atmosphere I lived in, though in most ways it had the same relaxedness of his grandparents' house.

At graduation he was nervous because his parents had come —he would go back to Huntsville with them—and he wanted to perform well, for his father especially. And he did give his speech without one glance at it. He had his career plan outlined too. "My father, order personified," Brand said, "insisted on that." Order kept you sane, his father said. "So my plan," Brand said, "is part-time at Kodak while going to Syracuse University, open a studio, or—" *Or* because, as we would soon find out, he would no longer have to commit himself, he would be free, he would not be obligated to his father.

His mother was obviously proud of him, blooming, tall but fragile in ephemeral white with a great white picture hat, reflecting much of Brand's own coloring, with a beautiful smile that she would flash with great sincerity but with an always nervous laugh. His father, as I expected, was officious, with that officer-out-of-uniform posture of one condemned to endure the social occasion. What startled was that he was dark, hair dark and eyes deep brown and skin swarthy, and could—it was a shock—captivate with an almost intense charm. At the grandparents' house he came straight to me and gripped my hand.

"Ferris, Paul has talked and talked about you—like a brother you must be—so you've been a real presence with us. And why haven't you come to Huntsville? It's a very beautiful city and rich in science, and with perhaps old-world customs not so harsh as in these northern parts. Paul will miss you. He tells me you stay here in Rhode Island to study—journalism?—and that you write well, which he envies because for him everything is visual, but is the world not visible for one who writes too? What else? Everything is visual. Not? And for science too. Even a theory must be sketched—circles, squares, parallel lines—or how deal with the imagined? But you know all that? Journalism, then. So you might even, you with your writing and Paul with his photographs, work for the same paper one day—anything is possible. But of course you must both be the best; otherwise, it is no challenge, not worth it. It is the best, always the best, by which we must measure achievement, as you, with your address—it was an excellent valedictory, yes, and your deep feelings against the waste of human life were extremely well expressed. Yes, the best—"

It was then Mrs. Brand intervened. "Heinrich, let Ferris have some cake." She took my arm. She was very discreet. "My mother," Brand would tell me years later, "would never say a word against my father." His mother, in fact, talked mostly about me, how good it was Brand had found a loyal friend who seemed even to put him first, "as he does you, a rare thing," she said, "you don't know how rare. Only good can come of it for both of you because there are so few things that stand up in the world, as you will one day find out, and friendship is one, though it can be such a flimsy thing, but a person has to hold onto what is . . . priceless," she said, "priceless, especially when you are away and look back and long for— But by then he will have—I should like to see him have—a good girl, a good American girl, because he is so of *this* country, yes. But I am being so serious—"

Not so long after, when Brand had found his good American girl, I would remember that talk, which heralded conversations —intense, nervous, revealing—that would take place between me and her years later in Huntsville.

Goya, Are You With Me Now?

The year after high school he seldom came back from Syracuse for long—a week, two, on holidays when he did not get to Huntsville, because as long as he was under his father's aegis, he still had to alternate vacations between Huntsville and Bristol. But before he went off, I did spend a quiet weekend with him in his father's "very beautiful city and rich in science." He had begged me to come after graduation. "Why not?" my mother said. "Let it be a belated graduation gift. How's that?" I knew Brand desperately wanted to be with his mother and in his own way desperately wanted to be near his father. Such dread of him could only reflect distorted love; and though he wanted me with him, I knew too I was a talisman for the moment.

But he did not remain long under his father's aegis—he quit the university. With his grandfather's help he set up a studio in downtown Providence. I didn't know until long after what a blow that was to his father (a direct blow? I don't believe Brand was aware of that at the time), though remembering his father's conversation with me at graduation, about being the best, I wondered at Brand's daring to violate his father's expectations.

At Brown I dabbled in art as elective and took a class the first summer at the Rhode Island School of Design. It startled Brand.

"But why so surprised?" I asked.

"Because you so loved the word—!"

I laughed at his mockery—he certainly knew his Bible—and said, "It's the same thing—images."

And to make my point, in his absence I painted a spacious canvas of an eye, his, and repeated in it an eye again and again and painted in each a miniature scene with people he cared about, imitating the format of Fra Angelico's five scenes from the life of the Virgin in "The Annunciation"—Bett, Emily, Clara, his grandparents, me—and presented it to him on his spring visit to his grandparents. Though the canvas was ambitious but crude, he swelled with pride, more in me, in my work, in what the gift meant and what the painting preserved of our high school years, perhaps, than with any vanity—he was surprisingly free of that.

"And my parents?" he said.

It was no criticism, but the question surprised me.

"But—"

Fortunately I didn't finish. His relationships, his feelings for them were at that time so ambiguous to me that I dared not. Had I blundered? If I had, his enthusiasm and gratitude quickly quelled any doubt or regret I might have had.

But I had blundered. Brand was right to be startled. Painting was not my milieu, and I soon realized I would end up with the hundreds of thousands who exhibit and sell their decorative art in malls across the country. I was not looking for a pastime, and I certainly did not need painting for therapy, though it did initiate a study that came to be a treasure house for my criticism and for those serious discussions with Brand, who was burrowing deep into photography—process, equipment, technique, history—and studying *with the absolute dedication of the novice*, he wrote, *discovering and absorbing the secrets of the great, secrets never hidden but always honestly exposed, which with enough scrutiny you can read as clearly as archaeologists read hieroglyphics once they've determined the code.*

More and more over the years—at the university and then when he had set up his studio in Providence, a stage in his development, an important stage, he claimed—he wanted to study the face. It was for him, he was convinced, the entry into "something behind the face," though he could not defend why he was sure ("Intuition?" he said). When I read that, I thought of his photographs of the bridge in fog, because he had said then too the fog might conceal something on the other side.

He steeped, buried, himself in the works of the great achievers, as intimate as a lover with their works. He could *connect* as if he were with them, whether with Julia Margaret Cameron or John Marin or Skrebneski or Mathew Brady, Hartley, the Bauhaus group, Ansel Adams, the myriad; and dissect; and leap from Cameron to Baron de Meyer or Walker Evans without transition. But it would be Stieglitz who most fascinated. It would be his wife who would initiate him into that discovery, and it would be a long time before he knew *why* Stieglitz, and it would be the Prado that would make him thunder with the realization of Stieglitz' failure; but more than to any other, something made him return to Stieglitz, "eat drink digest shit Stieglitz," he would say.

And surely Stieglitz, the works of Stieglitz, had had their part in what must have been his initiation into thoughts of suicide years before, though he may not have realized it at the time; and such thoughts must have been on his mind—for what reasons?—frequently over the years, I thought after his grandfather's phone call.

By his own hand, his grandfather had said.

Brand had spoken often of Stieglitz' work, and especially after he had married Esther; and mostly during those long afternoons we four spent on the beach at my parents' old place on Eastern Long Island, he and I talking while Esther and Sylvia bobbed and swam together; and sometimes with all four over dinner and drinks because Sylvia, no art critic but sensitive to harmony, as the jewelry she designed showed, was notorious for going right to the point, tenacious, *biting* at it, in fact; and years later, when Esther became the famous painter and Brand an internationally known newspaper photographer and they bought the large Victorian house overlooking the Providence harbor. They were thrilled with that house—Brand because he was close to a world he loved, and Esther because the house was perfect as a studio.

Those afternoons on the beach in Greenport were some of the happiest of his life, he would say after, doubly so because, yes, he had found his American girl, surely a far cry from the American girl his mother must have envisioned for him, not typical, hardly the "sweet and lovely" version of the popular song his mother would sing and then laugh.

He had found her on a visit to Huntsville, and he had known her at once. Her face stunned. Stone it might have been, so still she stood, he wrote me, sculptured—not beautiful but baffling.

She has an air of mystery about her. It's her eyes. At her stillest they startle like two creatures who never tire of observing the world—and everything registers, her face instantly takes on the mood of what she sees. I call her the woman of a thousand faces.

He included a photo he'd taken, one of the hundreds. Her features were bold, not beautiful, but odd, yet the combination made a dynamic harmony, and in that sense Brand was wrong: she was beautiful. Baffling too, perhaps. I couldn't know that then, but of course I was not seeing her with eyes of passion as he was.

I'm in love, I've met the girl, he wrote, *I'm going to marry her. I know it.*

I had to laugh: Brand always *knew.* It had all been very fleeting, a matter of a quick weekend. At the last minute on Sunday afternoon his mother had said it was the final day of the art exhibit at the Civic Center. They had all wanted to go (their neighbors, the Dietrichs with their daughter Heidi, his childhood friend, had had lunch with them). There was plenty of time before he had to leave, and they could go on to the airport from there. The woman, Esther Warner, must be exceptional; she was included in a spread in *Time* on the new generation in art, his mother had said.

She was easy to pick out, the very slim woman, svelte in a long sheathe, with long legs and long arms, which, he wrote, *speak with a special language, her words come out of her fingers.*

From your language, I wrote back, I *know you're destined to her, yes, destined*, and he would believe that, certain she had been sent, *headed all along right to where I'd find her.*

Well, he'd found her and he let her know at once who he was:

"I'm Paul Brand, I'm a photographer, I want to photograph you."

She smiled. She was dark with heavy long hair, dark. (He would be startled later to come upon her painting with a snood on: "to keep my hair from flicking over the oils and ruining my work.")

"Why, of course." And her arm swept out to encompass the paintings surrounding them.

"No, not the paintings. You."

I'm sure Brand was all glow. At his best he was too charming to resist. But he said she had wonderful poise: there was only the least hiatus in her hand—it stopped in mid-air before she lowered it to her side, still—and her eyes only briefly halted on him, perplexed, before she said, "Now why would you do that? It's my art that's important."

If it weren't for a compelling naiveté in Brand, he would never have managed his blunder:

"I haven't seen your art, but I *have* seen you."

"And you don't care for art?"

"More than anything. You're a work of art."

Brand said he'd never heard anyone burst into such spontaneous laughter.

She was intrigued, perhaps fell in with his wishes because she *was* intrigued. As we both would learn, she was completely self-effacing when it came to art, yet this had nothing to do with art. Perhaps it startled that, used as she already was to a growing reputation (she was some years older than Brand and had been married and divorced), she was reminded *so exclusively* of her person, reminded that the public reputation had not led to the private affair, that what he saw, if she could put it that way, was exclusively—or, as she did put it, *merely*—the woman.

They talked then—or *she* did, trying to learn something about him, frustrated because, as she said to those around her, "I can't get a thing out of this man. He turns every question back on me. 'I'm a photographer' is all he'll say."

"There's more—but I'll save it for when I photograph you."

I have to say his approach was original, a whirlwind reflecting a sudden momentary Don Juan whom neither Brand nor anyone else suspected had existed in him.

"And when will that be?"

"Anytime you say—and in Rhode Island, Providence."

"Providence!"

"My studio's there—and oh don't you worry, all expenses paid—so when? In a few days, next week, next month. *You* say.

Here's my card. No, that's not enough. Let me call you too. Give me your number."

She did.

Much later, in the Providence studio, she would tell me it shocked her afterward—though she never regretted it—that she had capitulated. He'd given her not the least moment to think, and his people were prodding him about catching a plane.

She cried, "You haven't seen the paintings!"

"I want to see all the ones in you you haven't painted yet," he called back.

That informal spontaneity was the American aspect that had rubbed off on Brand, but what had captivated her, Esther said, was the young man who could be formal, a gentleman through and through, and treat her with respect, courtesy, consideration besides putting her first. She said men so seldom went that far out of their way these days. Perhaps her first marriage was speaking through her words: it had been, she said, a disaster from the beginning. Between Jeff's passion for the stock market and hers for painting, with sex running third, they might have been singles rooming together. And Jeff resented her making "clumps" of money "without working at it" as *he* must to make any kind of haul on the market. What he resented, she said, was her sudden liberation—he no longer could reach out his hand and find she was there, dependent on him. "Besides," she said, "to be fair to Jeff, I was immersed, *lost* really, in what I was doing. He resisted any idea that my painting was more than a physical act. That was his supreme resentment. I think he saw my world as dangerous, so he refused to enter. He had to live with two of me, but he turned his back on the me that threatened him. So I took to living almost exclusively in my studio. That was in New York, at the end, just before the divorce."

She'd later tell me, "I followed a hunch, I always do." She went to Providence.

"My miracle days," Brand called that week. He took hundreds of photos in his studio, not only of her face (mostly) but in full form outdoors—at Prospect Park under the statue of

Roger Williams, at the railing with the city below, on the Brown campus, emerging from her downtown hotel (she stayed there two days and then four in his apartment), on the harbor docks. Those photos would become well-known. They would grace newspaper and magazine articles I myself would write about her art. Brand said, "We were two days inseparable. Thinking she'd vanish I gave her almost no rest. I was merciless, I realized after, obsessed. All I could think was *Esther* and *face*." The second night she said, "I'd like to get your breakfast for you." "What time?" he said, and laughed. "Whatever time you get up," she said. "Fine," he said. "I'd have to be there," she said. "Fine," he said. "We'd better go home then," she said.

Sylvia and I saw at once that Brand was lost to Esther, smitten, though not only by her sensuality. Her face and gestures conveyed an unintended and completely false indifference, which seemed to exude experience and both excited and challenged men. She was almost five years older than Brand, and in her "studio isolation" just before the divorce from her ex and in the year since, she had her affairs. But he was also smitten by a fascinating and perfectly natural way she had of letting a word, gesture, and object during conversation create a labyrinth of the subtlest chain of (you couldn't call it intellectual, perhaps sensuous) associations:

Oh, the coffee smells so good, Sylvia—Nigerian, is it?—like chestnuts they cook in braziers on the street corners in Paris. The smell alone can make you close your eyes and see the whole scene, street, houses, people, even the old concierge forever in the doorway of number 34. The chestnuts' round light spots resemble the shape of the nipples of the native women Gauguin painted. We shun odors, but the skin has scents of its own too, subtle secret scents you can distinguish from odors when you're close enough, though sometimes it needs your mouth, better your tongue, to feed your nose, a smell so rich it can make you halt the way baking chestnuts do with the sudden realization that perception is sensual too—the way it works I mean—you can almost draw the motion it's so fluid. You wonder if there's a secret pattern you're caught up in till the realization makes you break the flow, or is the breaking merely a shift in the same motion . . .?

By then Brand had not only seen all her available paintings but gone straight to the museums that had begun to buy her work and asked permission, with her consent, to photograph them. And he studied them. He studied them as if they were her body, her mind.

"Sometimes," he said, "I feel as if Esther has cut herself open and laid bare the core of her innards and penetrated what they *seem* to be to reveal what they really are. She's painted something that's there that you can't see. She studies what she paints in such detail that the *details* have lives of their own yet are part of the life of the painting."

"Wait a minute," I said, "*I'm* the art critic here. You trying to take over my job?"

He laughed.

"No, just the raw material of your job!" But he was smitten by the paintings. "Once I'd seen them," he said, "I felt I was already living with her. I felt I had to."

And once he *had* begun to live with her, had come to know the real Esther—as far as he (or anyone?) could—he came more and more to concentrate on the individual paintings.

Though he considered Bristol his true home and his grandparents practically his true parents—he had a small apartment in Providence, yet virtually commuted—for the next three months Brand startled his parents by frequent trips home. Huntsville he always longed for and dreaded—longed for his mother, dreaded his father. Now Huntsville became the seat of his double passion, though one impinged on the other—he felt that sorely.

"Bring her up to the Island for a weekend," I said. My parents' cottage was almost always available. "Sylvia" (we had been married less than a year then) "loves the Island. We can ferry over in no time."

He said, "How about a week at Easter?"

They came prepared, got through blood test and all on the

Island. Sylvia and I didn't know till they arrived that we'd stand up for them at the wedding.

Brand said, "I've called Riverhead. We're going to get married at the town hall."

I realized then why he'd chosen the Island. A civil marriage was a major rejection: his father would fume at the disregard, the lack of old-world convention.

Easter was cool, but theirs was actually, Sylvia said, a cozy honeymoon for the four of us. We walked, talked, drank, raked the beach for shells and polished stones. Though we'd had a church wedding, Sylvia and I had gone right back to work after the weekend we'd married. Sylvia and Esther cronied at once, perhaps because they were so different and in different camps and one's work complemented the other's, so no threat. And they admired each other both mentally and physically. Sylvia was small and fleshy, sensually quivery, with a figure just edging ripeness, ready to spill, with precisely the kind of appeal the world had for Esther, for in her paintings, vase, building, tree, beetle, weasel opened and spilled too, touched the other with a suggestive fusing so that it was hard to say, despite the sharp lines that *contained* her objects and made them seem so complete, that they had any *separateness* from the landscape around them. And to Sylvia, Esther had some of the same monumental, isolated quality of the objects she painted. She admired Esther's sculpturesque presence, realizing that her stillness when not painting was a kind of waiting for something or somebody to rouse and release that energy—it erupted in an excitement of talk or cooking or walking or examining a bud ("It's ready for *him* to pass by"), a painting, a rivulet, an alley ("like a sharp wrinkle"), wood grain, algae ("like an island in your eye, don't you think?"), the shape of a house, the colors in a spot of oil. Sylvia had a sensitive scent for drawing her out. Such complementing and mutual understanding were rare. The relationship would go on after both our divorces, and it would be a connection, a friendly network, we four would have ever after.

I had gone right to her paintings—because I wanted to *know* her, especially for Brand's sake, and because if she were of prime quality to publicize her. So almost from the beginning I wrote now and again on her work, the first of the articles for the *Journal-Bulletin* Sunday magazine—with Brand's photos.

"You write so well, Ferris," she said.

"Not so well as you paint."

"Maybe you haven't found your subject yet."

I laughed, but she was all seriousness.

"Maybe it's out there waiting. I have to find it."

"Perhaps not so far as you think. Things seldom are."

Her paintings were certainly testimonials to that: the snail you might miss underfoot, or dread, or scorn, appeared on her canvas enormous, beautiful in its detail, its shell the whorl of the universe, each fine brown dot on its flesh a universe in miniature, its probing antennae penetrating, its snakish slither sheeny and viscid as semen. Alone on the canvas, the snail became an enormity in itself, and the vast space around it implied the immensity of creation beyond the limits of the canvas.

"The world's your bible, isn't it?" I said to her.

The question bewildered.

"How do you mean?"

"The paintings are revelations—I mean they're *revelation*."

"I'm afraid that's too theological for me."

"But I don't mean theological—spiritual, perhaps."

"Are you telling me I have a cause, or an idea?"

"No."

"Are you saying I think when I paint?"

"No. You feel."

"Yes."

"But your feelings are visual."

"You're really pushing me too far, Ferris. I *see*, if that's vision."

"Now *you're* not pushing far enough, because you do see. You always see *things*. Vision is seeing into—far, and profoundly. And you do."

"Do I? I suppose I'm so used to my world—because I'm *in*

it all the time—that I don't think of it as anything *but* my world, so I never think of it as profound."

She was not being coy, but candid. There was no facade to her, no disguise of her art or self. That was an essential part of her beauty, a kind of captivating nakedness. Her candidness could disarm deceivers. That directness was one of the characteristics that bound the three of us to her even after she divorced Brand. I suppose most people would call it simply being honest or telling the truth. Sometimes it left you with not a leg to stand on.

Esther did not want to leave Huntsville. "Providence is ugly," she said. But that was hardly her reason. She could easily penetrate ugliness. She knew "fair is foul and foul is fair," if she knew anything. But the large studio her parents had built for her on the edge of their property on Monte Sano years before her first marriage—with an extensive and breathtaking view of the valley below, the woods and mountains in the distance, and, she called it, infinity—was like her own body, she said. She felt enclosed but free there. She feared—always—losing that visible state of mind, that green peace which so much natural surrounding created. But in Providence Brand had rented a second story and the attic, with an enormous window and vast skylight, in an old house that had been remodeled by a painter. What he knew would sell her on it was not the partial view of the vast open traffic space below and the city with the capitol dome off to the right, not the mass of green concealing the houses off to the left, but the view of the harbor beyond, the break of water, the distance, her *infinity*, and, of course, light. Though he rented it for Esther, the view appealed in an essential way to the photographer and it would be influential too in weaning him away from his photographic studio in downtown Providence.

Eventually they would buy the house, but it was Vietnam that weaned him away.

He—we—hadn't been drafted. At his own request, he was sent to cover the war. I saw him just before he left. My visit came at a moment when he was becoming disillusioned with photographing this or that face for whatever occasion—graduations, weddings, birthdays, public recognitions. From his talk I knew that he was about to give up photographing faces, though he hadn't thought of closing shop. Of course he was impatient, anxious, ambitious—we both were; after all, we were young, early marrieds, already lucky in the ease with which our particular talents had opened up paths for us.

We sat in the rear room, which gave onto the backsides of buildings, *a hive of sights* Brand had loved as any photographer might—faces in windows, a web of TV antennae, bins, people in windows or chatting below, trucks, laundry, trash, bums: what Esther might have found the world in.

At one point he broke into a diatribe against portraits.

"Portraits lie. 'Perfect!' the viewer says. 'That's *B* to the life.' 'You've caught something of B's joy or B's sadness or B's dignity in repose.' But *where's* B? 'Oh, yes, that's B, I recognize him at that angle.' *At that angle!* As if all B's life were that angle, as if it were possible to make of the particular man the whole man at that angle, as if by capturing the right moment the whole man could possibly be revealed, as if the impossible had been achieved. And then in minds the world over, that photograph *becomes* the man who is *not* that man, that limited man—the Carlyle whom Julia Cameron captured as if his head were aflame with the apocalyptic; Amy Lowell or Virginia Woolf smoking a cigar as if rebellion were the key to their lives; and, well, to exaggerate my point, the picaro Einstein sticking his tongue out at the questioning photographer. No, the moment is *not* the life. The moment does not capture the life. No wonder Pirandello and Sartre wrote plays showing characters erroneously condemning a man for *one* action at *one* moment of his life so that no other moment exists in our impression of him. We fix him forever in that moment. But a man is not that, and photography can't be that either and be honest. No, a man is a flow of moments so indistinguishable from one another in the unbroken rhythm of life that any static image is a lie unless it captures his complexity, even *if* that complexity could be reduced to complementary images of his many conflicting sides, and even that result would be a lie because . . . where's the illusion of the *flow?*"

"No," Brand said, "photography will be a lie until it can find a way to reveal the motion moving within the photo."

He said it not only with a certain excitement but with a certain pain, "Because that's the ultimate challenge of photography, and until this very day it has failed. And it's only by accepting the challenge that we can try to overcome its limits, because as an art photography is *still* limited. Nothing shows that more clearly than painting, though you can't make one art another and you can't really contrast them infinitely. Photography is photography, and painting is painting. Even when painting uses photographs as raw material, it doesn't duplicate photography. But painting succeeds in overcoming the limits of paint and the frame. It holds forth infinite possibilities of greater exploration. It's constantly accepting the *ultimate* challenge of the *ultimate*. And why shouldn't photography?"

But even in the Vietnam photos he had clung to the face. He had simply *moved beyond* to groups of faces, concentrated on scattered figures. Whenever he could, in the midst of action, he caught a face—part, profile, eye, mouth and chin, a tilted helmet, a fringe of hair in the foreground—or a head smack in the center—to deepen space and distance. His technique gave both immediacy and detachment. I raked over the media, always with the confidence that I'd recognize what was undeniably his.

I wrote him that.

Don't be a fool, he wrote back. *Some Joe Blow comes up by accident with a photo that puts all yours to shame. Then where's your work? Never underestimate chance, my boy.*

And I wrote, *So he does it once but can't repeat it. You do it again and again, and the work adds up to some collective view. That's the mark of a master photographer. Something's evidently going on in the emotions and head of the man behind the camera, and seeing enough of his work you can begin to detect that.*

Oh, if only you're right! Brand wrote. *But just now I can't help opting for Joe Blow's single photo.*

I wouldn't let up on the dialogue. *So what are you supposed to do? You're in the midst of a war. You don't sit in a paddy field waiting for chance to send you a once-in-a-lifetime opportunity and hope you recognize it when it comes along.*

That was unfair of me. I was ashamed because more and more I sensed what capturing a vision meant to him. Perhaps I goaded because I didn't see what he saw and didn't know fully what he meant so I prodded him out of my own inadequacy or helplessness, the only way I could handle it.

In the Vietnam photos women, old people, children, soldiers are standing right beside you. You're in the middle of action, yet you get a glimpse of villages, smoke, masses, mountains. In the jungle photos, shots are made as if he were on his knees or lying on his back trapped in an intricate web of heads and bayonets and weapons and legs passing through a suffocation of near vines and trees with no escape to the few shreds of sky barely visible beyond.

Some weeks before Lyndon Johnson made his famous end-of-the-war speech and resigned, Brand, who had been on a special assignment in Vietnam, called from Japan.

"Japan! There's a war in Japan?"

He laughed. "I'm a war hero, don't you know? I was wounded."

"Wounded!"

"Stabbed in the thigh."

"Bad?"

"Bad enough to be flown in with some GI's to a hospital here. I wouldn't have wished it on myself, but it was almost worth the shot *I* got of the gook flying through the air with his bayonet headed straight at me. If I ever saw lust to kill close up, those eyes are loaded with it. Somebody picked him off and threw his aim just as he let me have it."

"You can travel?"

"I'm dying to!"

"You'd better hop it to Madrid on the way home."

At sight of Brand I was shocked. "Look at you!" He was all

wire, so thin I was sure he'd grown even taller. "What'd they feed you on, shrubs?"

He laughed. "I look like one, don't I?"

Browned dark, he did.

Only the fire in him, his young skin and thick clean hair, all light, saved him from looking like a cadaver.

His face, thin, narrowed, was all eyes. Restless, they seemed to touch and probe as if everything were a bush, tree, enemy. His photographer's eye must have been sharpened by the war.

I kidded him: "Where'd you leave Brand?"

But he was serious. "I dumped him. He had the shits half the time."

I chortled at how he'd picked up the language.

"Nam made me respect my body like never before. It's all I've got to work with—me. And if it goes? And I'd never used it, no. Jesus, Ferris, a guy can waste his fucking life and find out too late. Not me! From now on I'm not wasting a minute."

"You never did, Brand."

"Oh yes I did—when it came to *me*. I was wasting me. I don't mean I'm giving up work, not for a minute, but it's me, my body. I could've brought one of those girls home with me— God, they know how to make you comfortable."

"You fell in love with a Vietnamese girl?"

"Hell, no, it wasn't love—"

"Sex, then?"

"Sex, yes, but—" He was serious for a long time. "More. Me. My body. Not love, no, but fucking. I mean my body's the only way, the only thing I've got, like fucking's the only thing you can depend on to defend yourself."

"Defend yourself?"

"Yeah."

"Against what?"

"If I knew, I'd tell you. But everything. Everything else goes. When you're fucking, there's nothing else. The mind goes too. *You* know. When you stop, the whole world closes in around you—too quick."

27

"Everybody wants to escape from something."

"Escape from? No. That's not what I mean."

"How in hell can I know what you mean if you don't tell me, Brand. You on drugs?"

He laughed. "I told you—if I knew, I'd tell you. But not escape from something—if anything, *to* something—because everything else, I *told* you, goes."

Now it was my turn to laugh. "Sounds perfectly normal to me. After all, you're married, you love Esther."

"That, yes. I love her. It was perfect for a while, sure. But maybe the love stands in the way. I never thought of that till Nam. It's too personal. Oh, I don't mean I didn't—don't— want it, wouldn't start all over again with her if I could. But, yes, it's too personal. Before Nam I thought of her all the time. I didn't think of anybody when I was fucking in Nam, nobody. I just let go. Those girls knew just how to make you let go, if that makes any sense, because they didn't care about *me*, just giving my body pleasure. What happened to me I once thought could only happen if you loved somebody, that you *had* to love somebody for it to happen, but you don't. I love Esther. Maybe I love her too much. What I feel for her may even have stood in the way of what I had with those girls. I don't know. I only know I had it. I found out what could happen to my body."

"And you're going to tell me so I'll know what I'm missing?"

But he was seriousness personified.

"It's not something I can describe. And you couldn't. But I had an awareness *after*, a kind of gratitude that I'd been taken so far and a sense of loss too after where I'd been. It's hell to have felt you've been somewhere but don't know where, isn't it?"

"Sounds like paradise to me."

"You would!"

"But you've always had such a power of concentration, Brand."

"It's not concentration at all, but the opposite. When we swam in the Bristol harbor, you used to say you loved to close your eyes and sink in the waves and let the current carry you—remember? Like that. You're not you, but the current."

"I get it."

He laughed. "No you don't, but if it ever happens to you, you will."

"Well, I'm certainly not going to Nam after it."

"Prick!"

"It would be worth it," he added, "though I'm sure you can get it anywhere!"

"Prick!" I said.

"Atta go, Ferris! You'd make a great soldier."

"Forget it!"

Even then I wondered at Brand's "sexual success," not for a moment doubting him because he was much too earnest. He had discovered something crucial—he was more *impelled* than ever. He would not—evidently could not—let go. I don't mean that restlessness besieged him every minute of his life. He could be too abruptly all joy, with that glass-in-the-hand recklessness of the tavern-drinking-singing German, though without a drop of alcohol—he could get drunk enough on the world.

But it was precisely that abrupt intense joy that I could now relate to his intense sexual joy. It had the same sense of escape *from* something that he always related to an escape *to* the other. Knowing his capacity for joy in those sudden glimpses of the ideal he had always tried to capture in images, I didn't doubt for a moment that his ecstasy was as much an *escape* from the horrors he day after day captured in his photos. With his temperament he couldn't *bear* them, he had to escape, and he escaped with that same intensity with which he worked, concentrating to the point of vanishing. He had cultivated that escape till it had almost the characteristics of the ecstasy that experienced nuns and priests induce to carry them to *the other*. I wouldn't for a moment have been surprised if I had come upon a Brand stretched out on flagstones, impervious to the world; but it would not be the priest's spiritual *other* he'd be staring at, I was convinced; it would be an escape to the *joy* that only his awareness of the *horror* could drive him to. Without the horror he could never have achieved the joy. It was a dependence on the terrible, *terror* itself, a dependence which neither he nor I, then or now, could explain.

"Sometimes what's in me scares me," he said.

"Scares you? Why should it?"

"The same way the gook scared me when he came at me—I'd swear his face was ecstatic at the chance to kill. His face keeps coming back. I keep seeing that look. Fear? Joy? I couldn't tell the difference. I've seen some of our own men stab and stab and stab. You should see the look on their faces—you wouldn't believe how many men want war, Ferris, even love it—and I'd swear it was fear and I'd swear it was joy. How could I tell the difference? Yet I could tell. I can. I hurt *him*, didn't I? And I enjoyed it, but it hurt me too. And I enjoyed the hurt too."

The *him* revealed too much.

His father again.

He couldn't wait for the war to end.

"You know *me*, Ferris."

I did. He was all get-up-and-go. The war had steered him deep into the popular consciousness. And he was changed. Though he talked *body*, he had changed not only in his physical appearance and in his sexual prowess—he was openly emotional and vocal as never before the war.

The war was the monster that had bitten him rabid.

"There's only one defense against the government's madness and that's for you and me and everybody else to be on the job and do it impeccably, never yield even in a storm—that would transform government into true government. So many people depend on you that you *have* to be there, right there, in *your* spot when you're needed or all hell breaks loose. I've seen chaos. I've seen the poor sons-of-bitches *at* their job, straight or drugged or stoned, when they didn't know their job was *struck* and they didn't know *who* their platoon leader was or if they *had* one or *where* they were or *what* they were supposed to be *doing* and *why*."

And years after the war he'd go at it, seek out the sick and dying vets, interview and photograph and collect those visual terrors in his book *Mr. Orange, Agent of Death*. He would be miraculously on scene at major national demonstrations. He would be at the unveiling of that black monument with its thousands of inscribed names and with those vets' deformed and broken bodies standing beside it with the caption ". . . but who to give us work to feed us?" He would take the most revealing photos of the Kent State shootings. He would pile up those thousands of photographs of the Watergate trials as condemnatory in their objectivity as any evidence. He would reap the most complete record of how the beauty and harmony of Woodstock disintegrated into collective calamity. And the year before he glimpsed that face in the prison in Atmore, Alabama, and attended that boy's trial and execution, he would cover almost all of the forty-three-day Gulf War. And even though he was against the tyranny of one nation's swallowing another in an instant, he selected his subjects to expose the war's absurdities and the vanity of his own President and his own Congress and his own General and his own fellow citizens demonstrating their patriotism by buying yellow ribbons to pin on the old oak tree or any old tree or doorknob and buying more flags "made in America" than at any other time in U.S. history to wave "America First" and "Buy American" and its mass of heroes played up more immediately than in another war and with medals endowed immediately en masse "received from the hand of" . . . and those patriotic males and females also victims of diseases unknown to them before the war but acquired in the Gulf, "one disease for another" or "spreading the disease." And all through the eighties and to almost the moment of his death he would take those countless photos of victims of that world disease AIDS, men and women and children black, white, yellow in hospital beds or in beds at home or at their desks working or "retired" to their own environment or being walked or carried or buried and which may even have been the cause of his finally going back to photographing those faces in which he had been seeking for years that face which somehow even the day he had first photographed the Mount Hope bridge he must have unconsciously envisioned on the other side.

He was the enfant terrible of news photographers.

At the outbreak of the Vietnam War he and Esther had bought the house in Providence. Dean was born during the war and by then Esther was carrying Rich. She and the boys spent summers and long periods in Alabama. Those visits always roused her roots and nurtured her creative impulses. "I'm fed by Big Spring and given flight by Monte Sano," she'd say.

Esther always returned energized, shut herself up hours a day to work. She loved the boys. Nobody had a better relationship with them than she. They talked like three grown-ups together, but she was quite capable of working for days calmly without seeing them. And Brand, who so saw her as ideal, confessed to me after the divorce that he'd suffered as much during those periods when she was in the house working as when she was with the boys or alone in Alabama. Even then, he'd tell me, "I *wait* but she doesn't come." Sometimes he waited days, sometimes a week, two, for her to come to him. Perhaps because he idealized her, he dared not insist, harry, offend, so he let her desire govern his, he made her the aggressor. In the early years he was certain he had chosen well and made her happy. The proof seemed to be that she came on torrential, with unpredictable rhythms, and, released, went back to work serene. Apparently he believed she *was* serene, balanced and happy in sex; and he told himself he was happy because she was. But she was not happy, she confessed to him. And he was not happy, he confessed to me. She was not happy because she wanted, had always wanted, she said, to *receive*, to submit to the very force she saw everywhere driving, which she finally recognized. It was what I had kept prodding her with in my early conversations about her art as what was driving her blood, driving her very hand, with its motion. Her genius was commanding—she made you recognize in any fish, marigold, Japanese beetle, leaf she painted what it *was*—alive—as you'd never seen it before. She felt that life. She wanted to feel someone drive it through her. She wanted to be *taken*. Though Brand would never have indulged in the pleasure of excitation through the vulgar language of sex (it was a semblance of the old European in him, his father's forms; despite his antipathy, he couldn't help reflecting them), Esther had no qualms in telling me she wanted struggle, she wanted to feel Brand struggling to master, and *controlling*, that force. She wanted to be made to submit to what he had to submit to: "To put it bluntly, I wanted to be fucked to kingdom come."

And it was then, encouraged by Brand's frequent absences and the continual calls and visits her increasing international fame beset her with, that the first of her several affairs began, the several before their divorce. Steven Andrews. Brand never wrote me of her affairs. He would never tarnish her image, but the casual and recurring mention of *the young painter Andrews* or then *Walt* or the *one who* was enough to arouse my imagination.

I knew Brand well, but you can never know anyone completely. Even though you are sure you know someone only *too well* or *because* you feel that or because sometimes you feel you are approaching such knowledge, you may even unconsciously back off, even turn your back with the illusive comfort of assurance in *knowing him too well*; and when the event comes which all the signs have heralded—the moment of climax or the end—you are shocked because what you ignored but expected has *actually* raised its ugly head and confronted him—and indirectly you. Ends, which are the wrenchings out of the old, are violent, worse when silently violent. You watch. Watching is wrenching, and wretched.

Brand was wrenched and wretched.

I ignored the signs, or was too callous to see.

Brand might have felt suicidal then at what he was gradually losing. Gradually? Perhaps there is no gradually. You lost at a given moment. *Gradually* is simply the process of the unbinding after that first moment. The descent? After, you retrace your actions. You try to track down the exact moment. There *is* an exact moment if you can track it down. There may be many causes, but there is an exact moment.

Between Brand and me there were periods of blank, but never longer than a few months. Over the years with the newspaper, through an obsessive industry more than anything else, early on I had begun to acquire an extensive network of outlets for my art criticism. To do so, I traveled a good bit. At first the travel was a source of chafing with Sylvia, especially as she could only occasionally take advantage of time off to accompany me; then a source of chronic crankiness—justified, I had to admit. She not only felt—she was—neglected. In a certain sense she was jealous. I understood that—we frequently are jealous of what we can't compete with.

"If it were a woman, yes, I could cope, put her in her place, but this— It's not the work, but the travel, and my isolation. You go more and more as if there *were* a woman, as if your work *were* sensual and familial and . . . I simply don't *know*," she said.

I wouldn't write Brand that. He was having his own problems, problems which I probably played down because of my own with Sylvia.

Now in my apartment in Madrid, pondering Brand's suicide, those problems teased, persisted, harried.

By his own hand.

I remembered the day I had made the visit to his studio when he broke into the tirade against photographed faces. I understood him well enough then to know he had—emotionally—already given up on faces. But it was some time after Vietnam, when the boys were both still very young, that I knew he had left Esther, long before the actual divorce—

He had stopped photographing Esther. There was a kind of death in that. He had cut her off, or felt cut off, or unconsciously cut himself off. That in itself—I should have seen it then—must have been a form of suicide because it was as if by ceasing to photograph her, *he* had already unknowingly begun the divorce, had silently confessed an emotional rift he had no idea would lead to the real divorce.

I was in Europe when the rift came. I had left the *Journal* some time before that visit and since then spent most of my time in galleries for both my syndicated column and my free-lance work and made irregular trips back to the small apartment in Providence I rented after the divorce from Sylvia.

I've closed the studio, Brand wrote, *though I'll keep the place to work in. I'm staying with the crowd. Out there. Photographing events. And syndicated. And by your old paper too, yes, the* Journal.

And some weeks later, he wired me in Paris *Divorced April 14.*

The brevity meant hurt, *bludgeoned* even. Otherwise, he'd have written at great length with details about Esther and the boys and arrangements and his feelings, and as always something of his grandparents and perhaps even of his parents.

I wired him *Come immediately* to my cheap little hotel on the rue des Capucines. That street, almost impossible to find—I had wandered into it years before—was narrow and dark. The hotel rooms were small with large beds jammed between the toilet, bidet, and wardrobe, with one window over a small table. Dark as the rooms were, after the sudden wide spaces and the prospects along the Seine the stillness and smallness made a hidden retreat for quiet thought and perhaps would give Brand an interlude of peace and some healing.

I told him that when I met him at Orly.

"No, it's you who give me some peace," he said. "I know where I am with you—as if Bristol were right here. You bring back—"

"No bridges!" I said, "unless—" I indicated one crossing the Seine. "—this one, a little smaller than the Mount Hope bridge, but it'll take only a second to get to the other side."

"You!"

He broke into a frenetic gaiety as we crossed.

If he was in no way happy, he was not sad either, yet there was a desperation in him. He was doomed never to conceal his emotional turbulence: his skin had broken out, though not so pathetically as when he was a boy—perhaps even the cells learn to shield themselves.

35

It was hard for him to talk to me intimately about Esther, not because he didn't feel intimate with me, but because he was so idealistic about her, about women. Because of his mother, I thought, who was, he said, so fine—fragile, sensitive, dedicated. Silent too. Suffering in silence, I always gathered, because she *endured* his father, whom she must have loved deeply, bound as she was to him. Brand must have been as bound to him, or why such fervent desire to break with him? As silent as Brand could be about his father, when he *did* talk about him, it was always with a kind of repressed fury that was also desperation, too emotional not to be as much love as hate, or hate *because* love, but a love that he sensed but did not understand, or understood but rejected, yet he must have known his father wanted him to be a model worthy of that kind of love he tried to bestow, as Brand would say, *in his way*.

Still he would intimate that Esther was quiet but sensually violent. She could *startle* with her language, demands, and abrupt desires for novelty. He let out tidbits, phrases: *wanted to try it . . . such biting . . . those words she'd want me to say . . . what her body could put into it . . . lose me she could . . . wanted me to . . . my tongue . . .*

He didn't want any of his talk to change my impression of her and mar my close relationship with her.

But in Paris he made me feel the undertow dragging him down, though I failed then to know what it meant just as I had failed some time earlier to gather why he had stopped photographing her face. I'm certain he was not aware of the reason then, or he would have told me, though I should have gathered why at the time, I should have gathered it that day.

It was one of those April days with a cold light rain that so persists in Paris, that sad rain that grays the city, grays the very air, preparing it for the quick rare joy of sun, when he and I were drinking Pernod at a tiny round table at a sidewalk café on the Seine not far from Notre Dame, listening to that rain soft on the awning when he made that pronouncement on Stieglitz:

"The most famous photographer of the century was a failure," Brand said. "Yes, Stieglitz was a failure. Fame does not conceal failure, Brand insisted, not from the artist. Fame does not pardon failure. Stieglitz knew. Only the artist knows how far short of vision his work falls. Nothing can console him."

Brand was not criticizing Stieglitz' work, though his was a mature judgment. He didn't say it in defense of his own work. He said it with a certain compassion, an understanding he could only have acquired through some difficult trials of his own as a boy. He identified with Stieglitz. Surely nobody had gone over the work, the plates, everything he was allowed to see of Stieglitz' work and methods. He had read the articles on the life, critiques of the work, gone over the history of the movements and the galleries. But if he were so identified at that moment with Stieglitz, with failure, I thought in Madrid, pondering his death (I took down my own volume, one he had given me, of famous Stieglitz photos and went over those photos he had so admired), he might then have had thoughts of suicide. But he did not suicide. There was still Esther, though he no longer lived with her. There were still the children. There was his work, a world to photograph, not portraits but men in action, the international scene. And after all, he had made his mark in the extraordinary collection of his Vietnam photos. So no, it was not despair over his failure as a portrait photographer, as he saw it, if that is what he saw, and it was not failure at the loss of Esther and the children. Besides, he clung to Stieglitz' work long after that moment in Paris; and he clung—he would never leave it—to Esther's work. He talked of it as we sat in that little café. He might have been Stieglitz himself talking about *his* wife's work, Georgia O'Keeffe's.

And it was Esther's work, I thought now, which had kept him from suicide. He was not yet through with her paintings. There was something in them that still bothered him, something in them he had to know, had to have. And it was that which convinced me now that he had *not* had thoughts of suicide then. If he had had, he had repressed them because there was something he was searching for. And whatever he was

37

searching for he must have thought was *not* in Esther but in her work because after, years after the divorce, even after I had taken him to the Prado and we had had that memorable day when he *discovered* Goya, he kept going to the galleries whenever Esther was showing. And it didn't matter where they were, there in the States or here in Europe and even once in Buenos Aires and once in Rio, he would find a way to see the paintings before they were sold. And at those times (rare) when he went back to his parents' house in Huntsville, he would go to her studio on Monte Sano if she was there and not in Providence or in some city where her work was being shown, ostensibly to see or inquire about the children, but really, he'd always confess to me, to see her work.

Yes, I realized now, he had not said *to see her*, but *to see her work*. And that preoccupation with her work cankered me now, as it had cankered over the years. Oh, he'd fallen in love with Esther; he'd fallen in love with her the moment he'd seen her in the gallery that day he had had to hustle to catch the plane leaving Huntsville. Yes. It was the woman, perhaps even the face, he had fallen in love with instantly. But, I thought now, it was not the *woman* he married. He had not thought or spoken *marriage* in all his hours with me then, hours when he had nothing but Esther and her work on his mind. What he had talked about was her work, how close he felt to it, how her paintings teased him, how he could not get them off his mind. So it was *that*, I thought now, the work, which had finally lured him, or the work because the work *was* the woman. The woman was not complete in the face and the sex and the conversation and would not be in the mother. The one part of the woman that could never really be uttered but could be painted was what he loved and must know, must.

So, yes, it was the painting Brand had married. It was something *in* the paintings he had married. It was what Esther had, what she showed in the paintings, that he had wanted to be near. Her paintings embodied her vision, but he did not want her vision, no. He had married her perhaps thinking by being

close to her, he would be close to the source in her, a source
which he felt in himself; and through her, through her vision,
through the painting of her vision, *he* might find the *way* to
express his own vision in photography.

But why then hadn't he committed suicide years before? She
had divorced him, he was no longer near the fountain of her
inspiration, he had not—he'd shown that in numerous ways—
found the *way*. In fact, he had stopped photographing portraits,
closed his studio in Providence, and, following his war experience, turned to the larger field—incidents, public events, the
world—and with the same obsession, though even then he
managed to direct his travels so he wouldn't miss her work in
foreign shows before the pieces were sold.

Ironically it was that very obsession in him, and perhaps the
foreign influence of his parents and grandparents—just as it was
my going to work on the paper and opting in my early years to
leave home to work in Europe—that had given him a certain
detachment despite his real involvement with our generation:
for we *flowered* in the sixties, burst on the scene in the wake of
the *Beats* in our rush *back to the land*, our desire to *undermine
the Establishment* by reforming it, directing it *back to the people,
all*, and always with the doctrine of a *love* shown by the *gentle
people* through those real *flowers* everywhere handed out in the
nation on the first day of spring as a sign and act of *love* and
regeneration by us *flower children* who wanted to *save the earth*
and restore politics as living flesh and education as a living
experience and to live the *soul* in music and food and clean air
and in all green life and all creatures *here and now* in Christlike
simplicity and no theology in a nation thus *restored* in a world
unified, a generation so dedicated that we would abandon our
bourgeois materialistic life for that faith and those possibilities
while the poor and the middle class and the rich went on living
in their stubborn American way, whose education and social
services and rights and attitudes in the same stubborn American
way we modified or changed—but oh at what cost to us children of the sixties, finally isolated lost doomed to personal

waste and myriad destruction, our faith reaping like all faiths its pariahs (alcoholics drug addicts criminals crippled psyches free-livers maladjusteds) rejected after sacrificing their all, social and war casualties, victims dependent on the very government they helped change.

Perhaps as a generation we were as driven in our search as Brand was in his lone pilgrimage—or I in mine, though unlike Brand I seemed only to stand and wait.

Always there came cards, notes, letters from whatever event he was covering in whatever country. I could make some flimsy thread of his life. He insisted. I was the *someone out there* he made contact with. I was his anchor in the land. By me he could measure time, his distance from the dreams of Wood Street, his distance from any ideal yet to be realized.

And always I was alerted for the AP photos, I followed the *Post*, kept an eye out for his work in *Time* and *Life*, *Newsweek*, whatever magazine or newspaper I picked up. Over the years there was a kind of reversion in his interests in a series of portraits—of Johnson and Lady Bird, of Nixon, of the figures involved in the Watergate scandal, of the law figures Jaworski, Sirica, and Ervin—all marked by his special style, those odd angles by which he tried to draw out that characteristic he so railed against as the limiting factor of photographed faces.

But these were the rarity.

And occasionally over the years I was alerted by his sudden voice, long distance, sensitive at once to his tone, his need—something with the boys? Esther? his mother?—and sometimes by as sudden a visit.

"I've got to see you. I'll be there tomorrow. I'll go over it with you then."

It was absolute need. It was trust. Those moments I knew I was becoming more than his old friend, putative brother—a father.

It happened when Rich and Dean were five and seven.

"It's my father," he said.

"He's not dead!"

"No, nothing like that. But he's at it again."

At it again might have meant anything. Brand had always insinuated, but like his mother seldom spoke directly against his father.

Whenever Brand mentioned *father*, Pavese came to mind: *Either with love or with hate, but always with violence.* Brand's violence was always latent, suppressed. Earlier it would have been the cause for a severe skin outbreak.

Once men must have spoken about God that way—with respect and fear, and sometimes with fury.

"It's about the boys."

"What'd your boys do?"

"That's just it! The boys aren't even responsible."

It was costing him to *say*, so I knew it concerned something he had never told me, and surely not because with me he was secretive, but because he knew if he ever had to tell me he'd trust me to understand.

"My father's found out the boys and Esther are part Jewish. A mark on a breast in one of the paintings got him into it, and he didn't let up till he'd discovered the *tainted* blood."

"But what difference—" I halted. I knew what difference it made: his father was the paragon of pure blood.

"Difference? He'd kill for his point of view. He must have! Would. You know that."

He meant the Hitler war.

"But in war, who's innocent?"

"Maybe it wasn't war. There are all kinds of guilt."

I said nothing.

"He's disowned the boys."

"Disowned them? But I thought he was proud of them. And your mother—"

"Loves them. She's mad about them. She'd do anything for them and Esther."

"Well, it puts you all, you especially, in a miserable spot."

"It's always been tension with him, but it's my mother it'll kill. Esther can take anything, especially for the boys' sake— she's tough though of course it hurts her. And even that would be somewhat simple, but my father can't let it alone. He wants the boys' name changed."

"He *what!*"

"Yes. Legally. Which means he wants to wipe out all trace of connection between *their* blood and *his* name."

"But that's ridiculous. It won't change the facts."

"Oh, but it will—for him. He'll have *cleared* his name of impurity. He'll have renounced all connection with that blood-line."

"But doesn't he know that's impossible?"

"What's impossible for him is to know that one drop of Jewish blood exists under his name somewhere in the world. With his beliefs that's almost suicidal. If the name's changed, for him that blood is obliterated. You get the picture."

For an instant I had a revelation of the emotional impact of the life at home which Brand had never fully drawn for me. Over the years, increasingly, he had given me inklings, but perhaps because it was more painful to talk and to be loyal to his parents than to maintain silence, he'd seldom dwelled on growing up in Huntsville.

"He insists Esther give the boys her maiden name."

"But they're yours! He can't regulate your lives."

"Some people never stop trying. He won't. He'll chew the bone till no meat's left. My father has his own way. Besides, Esther's world is Huntsville. Her parents live there. You know how insidious gossip can be. You can keep sticking the pin in until people can't take any more and have to do something."

"But won't they consider the source?"

"You have no idea how respected my father is. He's a light in the NASA community, and he's a figure in town—he's worked at it. The irony is that nobody would ever suspect, especially working under government conditions, which absolutely prohibit any show of prejudice on the job, how concealed his hate is."

Hate.

He had never said *hate* with *father*.

"But can't you—"

"Do something?" He laughed. It was bitter. It was scorn. But not for me. Though he said, "Oh, innocent you."

That startled, because I was so accustomed to seeing Brand as the innocent, but something of the Brand waiting there to be revealed had been released. He hadn't changed, but circumstance was playing on latent aspects in him which might never have emerged otherwise.

"He's disowned me, Ferris."

I was shocked.

His voice went husky. It was more than grief. It was a death. He was filled with fury, and despair. And an inexplicable loss. For a moment his eyes looked absolutely blank. But what haunted was his voice—husky, it was his father's, exactly.

I finally said, "Surely he'll come round—" but knowing I was on quicksand. "Won't your mother see to that?"

"No, no, not Mother. She's helpless before him, more now than ever. And the boys too. He loved them. And they were crazy about him. I don't know what it's going to do to them."

"Has Esther told them?"

"She hadn't when I talked to her, but she'll have to."

But by the time he got back to Providence, she had. He called me, said she had—had *had* to—because she and the boys were all ready for a holiday trip to Huntsville.

"The boys reacted in a way neither of us had expected of such young kids. Though they were both hurt, they're little toughs already and tried to hide their hurt from us. Dean said, 'Who'll we spend vacations with now?' It was his way of comforting Esther, I think. Rich said, 'He doesn't know how much he'll miss us.' Of course they were putting up a good front, and she hadn't said *disowned* and never harped on *Jewish blood*, though she'd never tried to hide it. When she talked to them about it, Dean said, 'So what? We go to Sunday school at the Congregational Church, don't we?'"

Their attitude gave Brand a relief. Slight as it was, their reaction was a boost. But it was Esther who took up the gauntlet—because Brand's father wouldn't see him. "He won't let you in

43

the house," his mother said when he'd called. "If he picks up the phone, he'll hang up on you."

Brand heard the *madness*, he said, in her voice. She wasn't crying. She was beyond that, distraught almost to incoherence. "My father has reduced her to that. It's taken years, but he's reduced her to that. I don't believe she has a thought of her own left." His voice went husky, again hauntingly his father's.

It was Esther who traveled to Huntsville, leaving Brand with the boys in Providence. She planned her moves well. She stayed in her studio at her parents' place, found out exactly when Mr. Brand came home each day, and on the day she'd decided to go called an old friend in the neighborhood to make sure Mr. Brand's car was not in the driveway so she could be there with Mrs. Brand when he arrived.

Mrs. Brand was horrified, though glad to see Esther as Esther was her, glad to get news of Brand and the boys, but frightened not so much for Esther perhaps as herself for letting Esther in and letting her stay, and frightened of whatever her husband's retaliation might be, though Brand insisted that his father loved his mother, who had developed a terrible emotional dependence on his father through his father's "careful cultivation of her weaknesses," Brand said.

Anyway Esther was in the living room when he came home that afternoon.

"You'd think," she said, "he'd come up against the Wall itself when he saw me. But I ignored his reaction. I said, 'I've come to talk about my family.' 'You're no longer a family,' he said, 'you're divorced.' 'You know better than that,' I said. 'In an emotional sense, Brand has never left us. We're friends. They're his children—he's with them now—and as you're perfectly aware they not only share our blood but they can't change it and wouldn't if they could. None of us would.'"

At first, she said, she actually thought he didn't hear her. Then she realized he'd started to mutter very softly like talking to himself. All she heard was soft sibilance; she realized he was speaking in German, still perhaps to himself. Then he turned on his wife. She shrank as if scalded. And Esther said, "You don't have to take it out on her. You discuss it with me. They're my children, Brand's and mine, and I think you and I can handle this situation." But Mr. Brand would not listen to reason. He stared, she said, as if she were mad. She had never known him to be still for so long, as if in a trance. Then he broke—raged, still in that murderously controlled low voice, in English, though his syntax broke down more and more, "You will not the name keep, not not not keep the name. I will to the lawyers. The way I will find. They will never keep my name, those boys, no, if my life it costs, if every dollar."

"I could have gone hysterical," Esther said, "but *his* going hysterical saved me. It made me feel I'd triumphed over his perversity by keeping a cool facade even when he finally hurled *Jew* at me and cursed all *die Juden.*"

As disturbed and frightened as she was, she rose, furious but controlled, and without another word to him left the house.

"Your father may have his way," she told Brand, "but first I'll have to talk it over with the boys. The decision will have to be theirs."

"But," Brand said, "they're too young for such an important decision."

"Now don't *you* start," Esther said, "it's their life, they're going to have to live with the name, and after this they may not want to. Have you thought of that? If they want to, *let* them, but first I'll go over all their options and the consequences. How's that?"

"Well," Brand told her, "you haven't failed with them yet."

She laughed.

"Well," Brand said, "that's the first good sound I've heard for some time."

She laughed again.

That night, Brand said, he spent with Esther. It was almost a return to his ideal. That night she was that.

In fact, for a long time after that he considered her heroic for confronting his father.

45

Because she'd had something else in mind. However, she never had to mention it to the boys. They seemed to have read her thought; they brought it up.

So if she thought *vengeance*, and she *had* (she'd thought of every possible way to castigate Mr. Brand and that wasn't like her, Brand said, though he admired her for her stance, which he knew she'd have held even against Brand's wishes), she did so because she was sure she was right, yet she'd never act against her own and the children's and his best interests.

But it was the boys' vengeance, though they certainly were not conscious of *vengeance*.

Esther did explain their options. She gave them their will, young as they were. "You may leave things as they are. You may change your name to my maiden name. You may change your name to any name you choose. Anything is possible."

"They were amazing," Brand wrote.

"We," Dean told Esther, "will talk it over and let you know."

She'd never had such a revelation of the boys' character or intelligence or love or even at that age maturation.

"We want to have a talk with you," Dean said. "We've decided."

"And," Esther said, "after a brief explanation of why they did *not* want the other options, Dean said, 'It's because we're proud you're you, Mom, and we're yours, and we're not ashamed of anything you are or we are, and Dad's not ashamed either, and we're proud of your work and your family and your blood, and you're smart and sensitive and we want to be like you, and we're ashamed of what Grampa Brand's done to us all. And we love you and we want to take your gram's name.'"

At their words Esther clutched them, and they held her tight. She had never cried in the presence of the children before, she said, but she couldn't hold back—she shuddered, broke, cried quietly, and didn't let go of them.

"Grandmother Friedman," she said.

"My boys," she said. "You *are* mine."

So they became Dean Friedman and Richard Friedman.

Brand, when he told me, almost quivered with it. He was pleased with the boys, but always too there was his own admiration for Esther's sensitivity, and it was as if he were proud the boys had intuitively recognized and chosen to identify with the source of her magic.

"A sign?" I teased.

"Of course!" He laughed. We could never forget our high school days.

But he was pleased despite losing his *nominal* connection with the future. The name business did not bother him in that respect. "The boys are mine with or without the name." But he was more than pleased, I knew, because he had dealt his father another blow. More than the name, that must have been his primary thought. The vengeance was not Esther's or the boys' but *his*, one which he himself did not exact but whose fruits he enjoyed but suffered precisely for that reason, though indirectly he could claim responsibility.

Against my father.

Sometime after the boys' decision, when all was legalized, his father would have received that notice Esther had mailed to him, of the formal change of the boys' name to Friedman. Brand must have realized that if such an act separated him further from his father, it also bound him more closely to his father, and his father to him. It must have gone on festering in them, so one was never really absent from the other's mind.

What was typical of Brand throughout the affair—even before the eruption—was that, though he had known of Esther's Jewish blood, he would never have confronted his father overtly with the fact. There was the strangest confusion between his desire to strike out at his father and his desire not to hurt him directly. He wanted to hurt his father, but he was afraid to. He had to hurt his father, but he hated hurting. He wanted to leave his father, but he couldn't let his father go. He was kind, but he had to betray his own kindness. He couldn't have love so he had to have hate. How much that revealed about loss!

47

H. E. Francis

Now, with Brand dead, I wondered if before he'd married Esther he'd known she had a strain of Jewish blood, if he'd expected a moment would come when his father would discover that, if Brand later realized that his father's hatred of the Jews unconsciously helped impel him to marry, and if at last his father would realize that his hatred for the Jews had encouraged that marriage which he would condemn as so despicable.

We all had to imagine how his father had received the news. It was years before Brand learned that from his mother.

Something else had happened on that last trip to Esther's to finalize the boys' change of name, though Brand didn't realize how involved he had become until he went back to Providence for his vacation the following summer.

I was in Madrid.

"I had to call you," he said. "I can't handle it unless I talk to you. I mean, I feel it's a sort of betrayal, and I can't stand that until you know."

"You're not making a bit of sense, Brand. So far, you haven't said a word. Come on now, slow down. It's not like you."

"It's Sylvia."

"Sylvia! She's not sick?"

"No, no, nothing like that. But . . . during the fracas over the boys' name . . . well, I'd seen a good bit of Sylvia then, and when I went away I kept thinking of her, maybe because she was alone too, and seeing her brought too much back, everything was so familiar to both of us . . ."

I knew what he was going to say: he'd been having an affair with Sylvia. They were together again—again, because he was back in at least part of the broken circle. Perhaps with all of them there—Sylvia and Esther and the boys—he'd felt the world of the past momentarily whole again so clung to it in Sylvia.

He did say it finally: "I've discovered Sylvia."

Discovered?

For a strange instant, despite the time gone and the distance from Providence, despite Carmen, I felt a moment of confused surprise, jealousy, fragmentation—but for only an instant—and

48

I wasn't sure why unless it was that word *discovered*, which might have made me realize I'd missed something that might have kept Sylvia and me together. Maybe my vanity was wounded because I felt imperceptive and not susceptible to whatever Brand had found in her. And maybe I was a little jealous that Brand had aroused a response in her that I hadn't.

But I had no right. Still, there was that unexpected invasion of the past, my past.

"Sylvia!" I said.

"Yes, she's a wonder."

"She always was. I'm glad you found it out. How is she?"

"Blooming. We both are. We're what we both needed."

Instantly I thought of Carmen, how the moment of need transformed the casual encounter.

I knew, once Brand had told me and satisfied himself that it had not disrupted our relationship, that was the end of it. After, out of respect for Sylvia and out of that loyalty he maintained to all connected with him, he never "went into" Sylvia with me or surely anyone else, including Esther, whom she was close to, though surely Sylvia went into him with Esther—they were that close.

Nothing was more clear than one night during the following Christmas holiday when I was in Providence on a visit to the boys and Esther. Carmen was in Cáceres with her people. After Sylvia and Brand arrived, the boys left and the four of us went dancing, always a rarity for us, at a place on the Pawtuxet. It was Sylvia's suggestion, startling to me since she had always been such a homebody. Brand hovered. "Anything you say." And how they danced!

Dancing with Esther, I said, "I had no idea she was such a little dynamo."

She echoed Brand. "Oh, she's a wonder."

Esther herself was going through a transformation. She said, "I swore I wouldn't talk art to the art critic, but *you* asked what I was up to so blame yourself. I've discovered stone."

"Stone!"

49

She almost guffawed at my reaction, and for an instant I thought she'd drunk too much.

"It has character. I've done nothing but live with stone. It's so alive. I spend half my time in ravines in Vermont and New Hampshire. You'd be amazed at how a ledge or a boulder takes on its life and seems to breathe."

She should be talking to Brand, I thought. I'll have to remember every word. This is the talk he misses. This is what his eye is jealous of.

As I watched him and Sylvia dancing, the thought cankered, ironically at a moment when he was so happy (was he?), perhaps because he had shunted what he'd always considered the object of his true happiness elsewhere. With Sylvia he'd become dynamically physical. He seemed to have fled thought. He danced with Esther and I with Sylvia, and we talked about our old gatherings on Long Island and in Providence, the days before the boys. We drank and laughed. Brand clung to Sylvia and talked. Esther, who needed little probing, talked not about her art but about her perceptions with a sense of quiet drama that excited. As the evening went on, and I drank, the juxtaposition of Rita and Brand and Esther and me struck as out of sync and made me feel displaced. I wondered if the others felt that and like me wouldn't mention it.

I said, "You make me dizzy with what you see, Esther."

"You're stoned." She broke into that near guffaw again.

"No, it's not the alcohol. It's you. You're enough to get a man drunk without a drop."

"Apparently I never was before tonight."

"Who should know better than you the importance of seeing the object in the right landscape?"

"Ferris! You would!"

That was our only collusion concerning Brand and Sylvia.

Their affair—it was genuinely that, constant but intermittent, because of Brand's work—didn't last, though it went on for almost two years and perhaps that long, Sylvia told Esther, precisely *because* of Brand's irregularity. The travel must have given the affair a sense of romance, of renewed novelty, of unwaning vitality which "permanent" marriage didn't suggest —a hold on youth, frankly. But, Sylvia told Esther, there was always his distraction. "He's mad for his work, it's his obsession," meaning she was not, she was sandwiched in—most of the time wonderfully, she had to admit—but then she felt used. "I don't think Brand even knew he was using me, my body," she told Esther, "but he was in some way isolated. Oh, we had such fun together. But we, our relationship, wasn't going anywhere. I felt *he* was, but I *wasn't*, if that makes any sense."

To Esther and me, observing them when the four of us were together, that had never seemed the case. But Sylvia was speaking from what wasn't the marriage bed—and to Esther, who would comprehend instantly from her years with Brand what I couldn't know except for the raggy ends of conversations with each of them. My conclusion was that Brand missed in Sylvia what had confounded him in Esther and what emerged in her work. Sylvia didn't have that vision to offer. He'd gone to Sylvia for the experience of sex he once thought had had nothing to do with Esther's work. Sylvia must have given Brand that *beyond love* or *other than love* so important to him in Vietnam, where survival was what mattered. Back, he seemed to be able to achieve another kind of survival through sex with Sylvia. He could *lose himself* in her, yet sex left him alone, isolated with what he must not yet have understood but desperately desired to understand. Perhaps, at least while he was with her, Sylvia staved off the feeling of helplessness that Esther could not help rousing in him.

Carmen said she and I were lucky by contrast. "How do you mean?" I said. And she said, "Every woman's thoughts sometimes wander to the idea of an intense romantic passion—or why else would any idea of Don Juan, though *he* was a bastard, exist? But when it comes right down to the facts, longing or no, she'd be pretty peeved if she didn't have her regular sex and everything that goes with it, and so would her man. We have that and a lot in common besides. Oh, I'm not saying you're perfectly satisfied with your work—you have your periodic disruptions—but they're certainly not the obsessions Brand has, if you're right about him. Yours—forgive me—is like the constant flame burning so low you're almost apt to forget it's there unless it goes out."

Carmen startled me. How much better she knew me than I'd imagined! There were echoes of Esther in her insights.

Carmen was more right than she knew. In my own work I was quietly constant with only the occasional symptom of some deeper than subcutaneous ailment that did not fully erupt. But Brand's ailment was chronic. If his skin only rarely erupted now, his body had always to be on the move. I realized that the dancing and his intense sexual preoccupation after the war, his energy with Sylvia, were merely two of the many immediate satisfactions staving off an ailment too profound to be disguised for long.

"Some people are born seekers," Carmen said. "It's their nature. The world's full of them. Some find. Some achieve fame. The rest of us, the millions, don't. We die unknown. Fact."

I admired Carmen's bald clarity. She was talking about Brand, but it pricked. I was there too. But, unlike Brand, who had to go *out there* seeking his prey, I was like a creature sitting in wait to ambush mine, though I can say I was hardly aware of that then. And my travels—unlike his, which were sporadic and sudden, governed mostly by social chaos—were to places of order, museums and exhibits where, though I might experience illumination, I knew beforehand what was there.

Nothing made this so clear as the afternoon in the Prado on his only long stopover in Madrid since his recuperation after being shot in Vietnam years before. Though I was the professional critic, Brand had the museum bug. He seldom passed up a chance, and he had his mania, that love-hate for painting.

A hurried visit to any museum of size, as any traveler learns, is enough to fuse and confuse paintings and blow the mind. But Brand had time, so we did it intelligently, rejected the grand tour and breezed under the central skylight past paintings and *salas* to Velázquez.

Goya, Are You With Me Now?

I was working on a monograph on a lesser-known Italian painter named Orazio Borgianni, so I wandered off to ponder again his three paintings in an Italian *sala* at the opposite end and left Brand with Goya.

Years before I had been startled by Borgianni's face staring at me as I entered the *sala*. It is a self-portrait, almost standard, with the painter holding his brush in one hand, the palette in the other, and staring straight ahead—at himself in a mirror? at some visitor? at someone sitting for him? The gaze is at once proud, defiant, concentrated. You would swear he had a will of iron. From the first I felt *comfortable* with that face, assured. It spoke to me of confidence and solidity, of a sense of place in his workshop and in his world, of irrevocable self-knowledge. I felt I had to know him and his world.

When I went back for Brand, he was still where I had left him, in the *sala* with Goya's black paintings.

"Have you seen the other Goyas?"

"No."

"You've been here all the time?"

He didn't reply.

Something had happened to him.

He was distracted. Abstracted. Stunned.

"Do you mind if I stay?" he finally said.

"Of course not. You know your way back, just up Atocha."

Brand was not one to talk, not until he had sorted out his impressions. In that sense he was ordered, very. He'd say he was born that way, or formed that way early. His father again. So I would wait. He would tell me in good time.

As I was researching for my monograph, he was left to himself a good bit and we usually saw each other after nine for the evening meal out. I expected a rundown on visits to Toledo, El Escorial, Aranjuez, the other usual places in the environs, but he went to none of them. And he was unusually silent.

"You've found a Spanish liaison?"

"You might call it that."

"You've been pretty moody."

53

"I've postponed my trip home a few days."

"Then you have found somebody!"

"Because Goya—," he said.

"Goya!"

"Is that so startling? Isn't that what you do—stay in Spain because Picasso, because Bosch, El Greco, Velázquez, Miró, or Borgianni—? So what's so surprising because above all Goya?"

"Come off it, Brand. It *is* surprising. You just don't postpone a trip because of Goya."

"You don't?"

I stared at him.

"I guess you do," I said, and we both burst into laughter. It was like old times.

"I have to stay a few more days. I have to satisfy myself. You understand that."

I did. It was not for nothing I chose to live near the Prado.

"I have to be near the paintings a little longer," he said. "I have to see and see. I have to *know* I can see them whenever I want to for a while. I'm afraid I'll forget because images fade and memory gropes in vain. Yes, it's Goya who's keeping me in Madrid. I can't tell you—listen, Ferris—I can't tell you what happened to me when I saw Goya's black paintings, only that the minute I walked into them—*into* them, yes—it was as if I *fell* and there was nothing to grasp to keep me from falling. And whether I stared at them near or far, I was *at home* with them, back in the same turbulence I felt and *had* to capture in my own photos. I felt the thunder in me because the paintings were thundering with that seething *inside* them. I've been back every day. I've lived in the Prado, but *only with Goya* and especially with the black paintings. I can't tell you now what the experience means to me, I don't know yet, but I will, and I'll tell you then. You'll know—yes, you will."

I could see how, beneath that talk, all was frenzy. He had discovered something—the Goyas were a revelation to him, and like revelation he could not articulate it. Not yet. But he would.

For a while the black paintings imprisoned him in himself.

That was understandable. The paintings are of unrelieved black vision. Of the fourteen, the three that stunned him like the Medusa stare involved masses of people. He must have seen in their faces parallels to his own photographs of masses in war or riots or strikes or worship or pillaging. He must have felt an affinity with what Goya felt in his own time, the same events, the same emotions. There is one of a gathering in the mountains at midnight for the witches' sabbath, and there are two of hoards of pilgrims dressed in black winding up the mountain roads to the shrine of San Isidro in pursuit of miracles.

He wasted no time before he left Madrid. He pursued Goya—the other paintings in the Prado, in churches and public buildings, in other museums. He even went looking for the site of the house Goya lived in when he was deaf, the Quinta del Sordo in Carabanchel on the heights of Cerro Bermejo between the Manzanares and the Navalcarnero rivers; but there were buildings there, no meadow, no gracious little house.

What moved him so?

What stunned?

Because for the moment Goya crippled him. Goya left him floundering.

It was some months after when he called from Providence. He wasn't floundering then.

"Yes, Goya kept me in Madrid. More than any painter he showed me the limits and possibilities of photography because at the same time that he showed me the limits of painting he showed me you could go beyond those limits. *Inside the photo* I believe I can *break through*. Oh, Piranesi with his dungeons and prisons without exits teased and tortured me. But Goya! I can't tell you. Nights after I came back I read Goya, the life. I found X-ray studies of the canvases. Did you know he'd painted the black paintings *over* beautiful paintings of nature and light and joy, the *opposite* of the black vision he covered them with? Two visions! No. Two sides of his vision. Two sides of the same vision, yes, the same substance, the same force.

"But staring into the paintings revealed most.

"It was the technique. You don't know—listen to *me*! Of *course* you do—what technique can reveal. Because vision demands a special technique. You can't invent it. Vision creates it, yes. Goya discovered it because he knew—I'm convinced he knew—he couldn't *shape* what he saw in men, animals, the world. Once I thought you could read paintings like hieroglyphics if you discovered the code. But Goya—he broke the codes, he plays against them all."

"That could be his coda."

"Maybe—but not in the black paintings. They're all streaks, smears, bold brush strokes—because Goya was trying to describe his feelings; he couldn't name his experience. He had to describe it his way. He was besieged by images the way a writer is—you; but he could only paint *around* and *against* space. He could only paint around what seems to be *nothing* but is in everything, is *everything*. He could only paint what it was *not*, *surround* it, suggest in vagueness, and create amorphous forms that would dissolve but remain only brush strokes the closer you get to them so that nothing is precisely defined, but the tension which the *force* moving them creates, that's there. Yes, you're left with the effect of the impulse he could *not* paint. You're left with the tragic formless shapes defined only by what impels them. He couldn't *define* it, but he *revealed* it. What he couldn't paint is *under* and *between* the strokes and smears—space. He wanted to paint the activity of matter. And how can you paint moving matter? But he *did*. He managed to convey the tumult in all matter, the terrible noise of silence.

"The light—is it *on* the faces or *in* them? The faces are grotesque, distorted, barely human. They're nearly formless, giant grubworms with open mouths. They're portraits of faces without reason, portraits of madness. He has caught the faces in the moment of their anonymity when they are most themselves. He has caught the irrational in action, caught it in such quick bold strokes it's no wonder they seem unfinished. The light is under the black too and the black veils it; it is *in* the density of the black too, yet the density keeps it from being almost invisible to the naked eye. Goya painted the persistence of light in those faces, but nothing could be more tragic than its waste in the pilgrim's unreasonable pursuit."

"And you're *not* a pilgrim?"

He stared, stymied a moment.

"I guess I am."

"And your pursuit's *not* unreasonable, I suppose."

"No," he shot at once. "It's perfectly reasonable."

"You dare to tell me you're not like the people in Goya's painting?"

"I certainly do."

"How then?"

"If I *am* one of those people in Goya's painting, it's only because I'm looking for something; but *what* I'm looking for is a photographic technique, which means I'm more like Goya in trying to solve a problem."

"I see. I know exactly what you're saying. But I don't believe you, Brand."

"Don't believe me! You think I'm lying."

"In a way, but let's call it misstating yourself."

"How?"

"Because you want the impossible."

"And what's that?"

"You want to know what's moving. You're one of those pilgrims. You want a miracle. You want to catch what moves light and dark. Don't you? You think you're reasonable, but didn't you say reason's just a part of that madness too? You're trying to control your desire and direct it, aren't you?"

"No! I want to be able to make the camera do what painting does. I want to make the light do what I *see* that it does."

"And what *does* it do?"

He was stymied again.

"If I could say it . . . I wouldn't be a photographer. If Goya could have said it, he wouldn't have been a painter. We all try to speak in our own form—and you, you image in words."

"But about painting," I said.

57

He stared at me for a long time.

"You mean about other people," he said.

"Paintings," I said.

"No, painters."

"Yes."

"Certain painters?"

"Yes."

"And why them?"

"Why?"

"Why not others?"

"Naturally because they've captured me."

"Captured you! But what's captured you?"

"What's in their paintings."

"Ah, then you *know* what's in their paintings?"

"Know? I'm trying to delineate—"

Brand cackled, actually cackled at that.

"*Trying to delineate.* You! You don't even know what you're saying. Trying to delineate what?"

"What's there?"

"What's *in* you, you mean. What's attracted you to them, you mean. Trying to find out about *you*, you mean."

"You think that?"

"*Yes*, I think that! And do you know why?"

I laughed. "You're going to tell me?"

"Because you can't talk about yourself without images, you reveal yourself through them. And why? Because you haven't found your own image, your own way to articulate about yourself."

"I had never thought of it that way."

"You will."

"You really think so?"

"Yes."

"Why do you think I haven't?"

"You have, but you've done it through painters so it hasn't plagued you, but a time may come—I believe it will—when painting and painters won't be enough. They won't take you far enough into yourself. You'll have to find some vital way to express yourself in your own images. Nothing has driven you to do it yet. Nothing has obsessed you."

"Maybe it never will."

"I can't believe that. You're too curious."

I thought again of Esther's saying I hadn't found my subject, but I was comfortable feeling I had by now lost myself, and not unhappily, in the labyrinth of museums I had come to love.

But Brand was lost. He was lost to Goya. The measure of his being lost was his persistent pursuit of Goya for months after—years actually, because he would never relinquish that pursuit.

Perhaps the pursuit, in the way in which obsessions sometimes help, saved him—at least for a time.

In Huntsville Brand collapsed.

On the telephone he said, "My father died. My father died. My father—"

He could say nothing else.

His mother interrupted. "Paul wanted to tell you himself. He wouldn't let me. He can hardly talk. But the doctor says he'll be all right. He wants you. You can come?"

"Tomorrow," I said.

"Best you come."

By the next night—New York, Atlanta, Huntsville—I was with him.

His grandparents of course were there. Their presence was a comfort, though at first it disoriented, perhaps because I had never associated them with Mr. Brand. It occurred to me then that I had never heard them mention him.

"Paul was—how you say—stunned," his grandmother said, "a kind of nervous breakdown, but he's somewhat better now."

"Because he knew you were coming," his grandfather said.

Brand gripped both my hands. "You. I knew you'd come." He sank back in the bed. But his eyes were restless on the window. "He went," he said. "My father went. He didn't wait."

After all Brand had told me about his parents, what was

remarkable was Mrs. Brand's composure. Though she had always that look of distracted concentration, she let no one manage. She was all order—managing the cleaning girl, the meals, the grandparents' and my comfort, the funeral arrangements, Brand, and the doctor.

Whatever went on in his mother, some steel in her held her together throughout. Had she been needing—subconsciously expecting—this all the years in order to become who she really was? Or was it to continue *him* after his death, to show in some private way that she did not betray his sense of form?

Brand, impeccable, rode to the church between his grandfather and his mother. Throughout the ceremony, he was mute, frozen. But at the graveside, standing between his grandfather and me, I could hear his throat, and at a glance from his grandfather, who slipped his arm under Brand's, I did the same, and just in time, for I felt the pull of his body: the grave pulled him, he wanted to go forward, and he let out a little moan when they tossed handfuls of earth on the coffin. His grandmother, always so perceptive, took his hand and lay a clump of earth in it and helped him toss it.

After, he retreated to bed.

"It's all that travel too. He never lets up," his mother said. "He never could do anything without concentrating too hard."

He was weak, feverish, and his face broke out worse than it ever had in high school, as if everything in his system revolted this last time, supremely, to rid himself of his father. Though he was thirty-seven then, it was as if he had become the boy again.

And how his mother tended him! Perhaps it saved the moment for her too, got her through the two weeks or so it took to get Brand on his feet. Besides, his grandparents stayed so she wouldn't be alone, and with them there and his grandmother making him *Linsensuppe*, *Kartoffelpuffer*, *Rouladen*, and *Kohl und Pinkel*, *Hammelfleisch*, and always *Apfelstrudel*, and other favorite dishes, Brand and I half felt we were in Bristol. "Food," she said, "marries you to the earth. You're never so close to the elements as when you take food in."

I was with him almost constantly. He was so often silent that I did the talking or read to him. He liked that; he relaxed then. It was my voice, I think, which canceled out time and returned him, us, to the illusory idyllic world of Bristol. Until then I hadn't realized what a prolific reader his father must have been. His library was composed of a rich variety of books—he'd been no ordinary engineer and military man—and some of the books bore his family's crest. On one of the first afternoons his grandmother had brought us her "famous" *Teekuchen*, and as Brand was dunking I saw a small book tucked half under his pillow and picked it up and flicking through it caught sight of a passage underlined in red so I turned back. *Rottet alle die Viecher aus*, it read. When Brand looked up, he bolted. "No," he said, and put his hand over the book and closed it and too firmly drew it from me, with shame and some anguish it seemed to me.

"It's a book he liked," he said, "though the author was a Pole, 'but an aristocratic Pole,' he said."

He slid it back under his pillow.

For a moment I puzzled over that phrase *Exterminate all the brutes*, but I thought little more of the incident then.

Most of the time Brand was silent, staring, but when he broke, his talk came in spurts though lucid. All that time never once did he utter *father*. But he must have had his father on his mind because *Dark*, he said, *black*. All he said was *black*, *dark*.

"My dark room," he said, "its pinpoint of light. *He* made his own room dark, surrounded himself by darkness, painted over those sunny pastoral scenes, blacked out that sun and green and joy for dark and flesh and madness."

Goya. He was talking about Goya. I had expected in his collapse an eruption about his father, but he deviated, he could talk *Goya* for *father*. It would be long before he would come to that outburst about his father. It needed time yet to distill.

I didn't realize until then the profundity of the impression Goya's black paintings had made on him. His father's death intensified the impact.

Sometimes he would take to whispering to himself in my presence, or to Goya:

"Surround by darkness. Surround *what* by darkness? Paint yourself in . . . Is that what you do? . . . paint only for your own eyes, to be able to live with it? What's *in* you that you're painting over? Is it so powerful you have to paint to bear it? Why hold the light back? Why paint light black? No mirror was as good as your eye, Goya."

At other times it was to me he spoke directly:

"Listen, Ferris. Goya turned his eye on the monsters. He *saw*—"

He would go blank.

"You see it. Isn't that enough?"

"Never. Nothing is. It's not only seeing, it's how to grasp what you see—I want to."

"You'll find the way to."

"Yes, yes, I will! Must."

Goya.

He said, "In Madrid I went looking for his house, the deaf man's house— You remember?"

"The Quinta del Sordo. I remember."

"I stood near where they said it might have been, on the Goya station on that spot, the city's built up around it. I tried to imagine *deaf*. I tried to imagine the house, imagine I was inside it, imagine the view, imagine looking out on it, seeing but not hearing what moved out there—the people passing, sometimes stopping at sight of him in the window or the garden, sometimes jesting or jeering or scorning him. Carts, horses, but no sound unless chafing and reverberations. Wind moving the flowers, grass, soundless. Rain. Even thunder muted to breath. And Goya cut off. Can you imagine *cut off*? A terrible torture hearing nothing, nothing, maybe an anonymous rumble— enough to drive you to madness. Deafness drove him into dark, and the dark's madness itself."

His insights were devastating. They frightened me. They made me, me the art critic, feel inadequate.

I said, "Don't let it drive *you* mad."

"Me! Ha! Goya's deafness gave him his ultimate vision. *His* triumph has saved me. He's pointed the way."

He believed that. He was elated with an elation which, though it might seem perverse, was perfectly natural given the moment. And his meditations on Goya's achievements, which had given him such insights, did help get him through the trauma of his father's death. They gave him hope. He was sure that if Goya had found a way in painting, he could find a way to break through what he saw as the limitations of photography. And that hope helped him recuperate.

I could go back to Madrid then.

"I'm going with you!" he said.

"You are well enough?" his mother said. "You are sure?"

What surprised, with her temperament, was how careful she had been not to impose.

To see the Goyas, he told me, and it *was*. But he also had to leave—he couldn't survive in that house, he couldn't live *father*, he would suffocate. The absence said *father*, the silence said *father*, *father* filled the house.

Carmen was thrilled to have him. They were like kids together. Carmen brought out his funny bone. Days, while I wrote, they went meandering through the Retiro, along the Castellana, through the Palacio Real, the Rastro, art galleries, the Casa de Campo. Nights we haunted the Machu Picchu, El Locro, other favorite restaurants, and since he could catch enough Spanish we took in the plays at the Teatro Español and the Olympia and the Mirador, and weekends after a *trasnoche* dubbed movie we dredged the all-night Chueca district till he'd danced to oblivion.

"You'd think I'd be exhausted, but I feel—like Bristol."

Home, Brand meant, back, young.

More. Looking back now, I saw he was *placed* then. My presence gave assurance. For him, I was that happy time, that place. He depended. A certain peace returned when he was with me. Then Brand could place *him* too, his father. He could know where he was and see his father with relative detachment. He

63

had his grandparents, but he had me too, his friend and his companion who would become, yes, his father when *no* father.

His anchor.

"Ferris," he said, "you don't know freedom because you've been free from the beginning. Here I can breathe as I never could there with my father. You don't know *stifled*. At the end of Hitler's war it was, as everybody knows, politics: the fate of Von Braun and his team was to work not in Russia but in the U.S. Nothing made sense, my mother said. What we Germans believed or what the Russians or Americans believed had nothing to do with it, only what the team *knew*, she said. You were bought or sold or bargained with, she said, but it *made no difference*, she said, because you yourself were *nothing*. All belief, on all sides, concerning us, was gone, she said. And the atomic bomb, she said, destroyed many people's faith in eternity. We were pawns. Any fool could see that, my mother said. Your father hated, hates, the U.S. He preferred to see the Von Braun group go to Russia. But any fool would know that it was not a matter of ideology. We were pawns—to a dream. Yes, Von Braun had a dream. *Where* the dream might be fulfilled was the thing of supreme importance. And who could blame him? Ideologies come and go. Politics are momentary expediencies that allow you to put something into operation, and the people have little say about what may or may not be more important than politics. And what do you do when you are caught in madness? Because reason demanded the insanity of shifting your faith, *in one instant* shifting from faith in one thing to apparent faith in another, which is to no faith at all."

His mother would go on like that, Brand said. He was proud of his mother. Such talk kept her sane, he said, for she was highly intelligent, and such talk was the line she walked between sanity and insanity, Brand was convinced. The problem was there were so few she could talk to *in that way*. Brand was one of the few. It must have been a nightmare for her, he said, when he had gone to Bristol to live. But in her heart she must have been glad he was gone:

64

"She didn't want me to be as nervous as she was," Brand said. "She wanted me well. She wanted me to triumph on my own in my own country. She was nervous all the time she was carrying me. It almost drove her mad, she said, when she found out she was pregnant at Peenemünde. 'How could I have let this happen to me *here, now?*' For the Americans had come, Germany was under heavy bombardment, they were bombing out all the camouflaged missile sites. 'They were all around us,' she told me. 'I did not sleep, I had nightmares about you, and then it was Peenemünde itself, I was sure I would have a miscarriage or be killed, and then it was over, we did not know what would become of us, I did not know what would become of you, and because the bombings drove me near mad I was petrified you would be born defective. After you were born I could not stop going over ever inch of you, your eyes mouth ears, I couldn't wait for you to teethe, walk, talk, afraid some defect might appear later.'"

Over the years Brand had had no desire to marry again, nor had Esther. Perhaps they still loved each other in a way they could not utter though that seemed doubtful to me, both being in one way or another very expressive people, yet they shared something deeper than a divorced couple's friendship. They still saw a good bit of each other when both were in Providence. And at such times, despite Esther's lovers, they appeared frequently together in public. Like him, she moved about, though she settled for periods in different places to paint—Alaska, Mexico, Argentina, the Hebrides. Though Brand was well-known among newspaper photographers, Esther had become internationally famous as an original artist, something which the feminist movement seized on and touted, something they but not she needed, for she could further their cause. But from the beginning she and Brand had been careful to keep the boys out of the limelight. There were almost no news photos of the four of them or of the children alone, no stories about the sons as children or young men. And it was not merely Brand's determination that their early years, unlike his own, be as absolutely free and private as possible, but Esther's understanding and will, for she understood only too well Brand's early life. It may have been there that both their problems and their bond lay. Esther was kind. She would never have violated Brand's sensibility or any causes she was aware of—she always spoke highly of Mrs. Brand, and out of respect for Brand's sensibility never spoke against Mr. Brand, though she had just cause after his disowning the grandchildren because of their Jewish blood.

"There's always a hurt in him, Ferris. I'm aware of it when he's with me—worse, after he's gone. Oh, not that we've lost each other—we haven't, we're the best of friends, he's attentive and absolutely dependable. I suppose it's my awareness that there's something I can't give him. I say 'worse after he's gone' because it's obvious that the Vietnam girl and Sylvia and I don't know how many others couldn't either. His discoveries and joys are momentary, like most people's of course, but not satisfying because he keeps thinking they'll lead to something—but he doesn't get there. He's like somebody maddened by not being able to solve an unsolvable mathematical problem. Sometimes . . . in a rare instance . . . when he looks at me, so lost—desperate, really—the sensation is almost frightening. I feel he'd like to thrust his hands into me and pull out what's there so he could know what's inside, because he *sees*, Ferris. I don't know what or why or even how, but something's hanging over him, it won't go away, it impels him. I suppose he doesn't know what it is. The hell is he can't speak of it. How can you talk about it when you don't know what it is? And Brand *can* talk, and brilliantly, once he's thought it out. I used to think that's why he wrote to you so often—because he was trying to figure things, or himself, out, and the writing made him make it clear to himself so he *could* talk. In one sense it amounted to a kind of confession. You were his father-confessor."

Whatever I had been to Brand, there was never any of that despair between us. We were at home together. We were re-vivified. Perhaps we were always those two high school boys in Bristol. We carried those years, and they came alive and advanced with us with no hiatus in time whenever we met.

Even in high school Brand was proud to have been born in the United States, where the many meanings of freedom existed side by side and in greater harmony than at any time in history, though sometimes it startled how tolerant other nations were on issues that our own was still battling over—and ferociously. He deplored the animal ferocity that came into play in the name of reason whenever reason broke down, so men broke down.

For more than a decade before the Gulf War, he had caught in photos housewives and workers and Catholic priests and Protestant pastors and professors and politicians and engineers and businessmen and clinicians and clerks disagreeing, actually fighting, over abortion.

As a contrast to home, I would hold up to Brand Spain's tolerance in the matter and describe Carmen's shock at the fighting over abortion. "Nobody," she said, "should possess my body, nobody my child, or my right to decide about either one."

"Brand," I said, "except for the women who want abortions, I think both sides are fighting for the religion or politics they *say* they believe and live by, and surely both sides *believe* they do, but do they? Most people go to law or Jesus only when nothing else works. But otherwise—?"

To be fair to Brand, I have to say he was not pleading for *his* side. He had his strong feelings against war, for abortion, and on crime or any issue. His photographs spoke eloquently in their own right, but they were not pleas either. He was long since beyond that. More and more he wanted to reveal wherever he perceived it that raw passion which was the same whether it spoke eloquently or depravedly through men's actions.

"If—here I go again—we used our heads, my god!—" He tilted his own back and broke into a gale, but it was not joyful, it was sardonic. "—look at them!"

He spread his latest photos of abortion riots, this time in Ohio.

They were photos of arms grappling and battering, bodies

being trampled on and beaten and dragged and shoved into paddy wagons, bloody faces—and in some photos buildings surrounded or broken into or burning.

"Who wants to kill if he loves life? Some of them—few—are there *just* to kill if they can. There are always those, but the others are overwhelmed by passion and at that moment they could kill too."

I saw his despair as he stared at his own photos. I understood it. Who hasn't had his emotions threaten to break out into physical violence?

"Sure you want a chance to create life, but if you could travel to India and South America and Africa—Somalia alone—you might come to terms with so much dying . . . if you were reasonable. Listen to *me*!"

He laughed again, this time sardonic too, but almost to himself, at himself.

"I'm reasonable. But *am* I?"

He laughed, sardonic again, to himself again.

"I've seen them die by the thousands. Why not fuck more kids into existence and see how many will die of starvation and disease? Why limit the number? After all, we're reasonable, aren't we? Of *course*. It's why we do everything too late, isn't it? We're artists at reasoning away the truly reasonable. . . . That makes us insane, doesn't it? And if one man should stand up against us for our own good, let our *collective* reason tell us to ignore him, surely many heads are better than one, he must be crazy, a mad prophet. Mad Galileo and mad van Gogh and mad Woodrow Wilson and mad Jesus and mad Martin Luther King. Mad, yes. But prophet still."

He flung his hand over the photos, spreading them over the table.

"Maybe if we barraged the world with giant photos and pasted them on walls everywhere, we'd see the results of our own madness."

"We do that," I said, "and it does help."

"In relief, you mean? Money, food, clothes, shelters, nurses, doctors? Charity. Wonderful! I don't question it. But horror doesn't *dent* us; it doesn't make us turn on ourselves and face what's in us. And *no*, Ferris, I'm not talking theory. I'm talking me and you. When they die, we die—and after we've dreamed kids, fucked kids into life— In photos you don't *see* far enough. You have to experience the actual sight. There's something behind the photo you miss. So what good are my photos if I can't—"

He swept his arm over them again, this time casting them in all directions over the floor.

It was one of his rare outbursts—rare because only in recent years had he let go like that and with shorter periods between eruptions. In some way closing in on himself. Though he was talking to me, his sounding board, he was really carrying on a dialogue with himself.

"Your photos," I said, "are as much a testimonial to our time as anything I know."

He had started very young, in the sixties, and even before he was cut off *by his own hand* his portraits and photos had become a history of the seventies and eighties and into the nineties.

"History! History's only a facade . . . our invention, history. I want to record something that's *not* our invention."

"Like . . ."

"Ah, we come back to that. That's my problem. It must always be *like* something. I must always find the picture that will suggest all it is."

"The bridge?"

He laughed warmly, nostalgically. "The bridge."

"You mean, you want to photograph the invisible."

"The invisible moving *in* the visible—exactly!"

"Except that you can't see it." I didn't mean to be facetious about the paradox or irony, merely factual, but it didn't bother him.

"Can! I can, you can, anyone can—at the right instant, in just the right configuration. Sometimes I'm so sure I've captured in an extraordinary photo the most common denominator in

H. E. Francis

everything, some complex motion so basic it must be simple, the root—but when I look at the photos, it's not there, I've failed. I . . . How is that, Ferris? How is it . . ." He looked at me with absolute bewilderment. "How is it I can see something and not be able to photograph it?"

"Because your eye does what the camera can't do."

"I should be able to *make* the camera do anything."

"Not the impossible."

"That too!"

"Only the imagination can do the impossible."

He went silent.

"And when have you seen the camera do the impossible? In whose photographs?" I said.

He knew—knew before I asked it—there was no one.

"That doesn't prevent *me* from doing it," he murmured, gazing vacantly. Then he looked up at me and in an abrupt turnabout so typical of him shook his head as if tossing off a pest, and smiled. "Does it?"

That cryptic smile was his way of terminating the conversation and enclosing himself with the challenge. His work was unquestionably important in communicating social conditions to the masses who read newspapers and magazines, and if he had gone that far, couldn't he go beyond the social to reveal something larger and all-pervasive?

But even when despairing he could break into a laugh at himself.

"I understand the dog—he chases his tail, fails, goes at it again, fails, doesn't give up, the poor bastard."

By the time of the Gulf War he had been in the center of enough major national and international hot spots from Cape Town to Sri Lanka and seen not only himself but the world as a dog chasing its own tail. "It never learns." His experience made him certain men couldn't change what was in them. "We curse madness in other men, but being irrational's our essential nature—we won't learn how to let it out. We repress it till it erupts and destroys us."

Goya, Are You With Me Now?

Brand was in Baghdad, covering the Gulf War. Saddam was burning Kuwait oil fields to keep them from the allies.

If this isn't madness! The sky's black, the air and land and buildings are so black this is Hell itself, Brand wrote. *Who was it said "darkness visible"? You'd think the troops were Satan's fallen angels. If I can find out where Dean is, I'll try to get to him.*

Dean would have no truck with ROTC shit in the university, but was called up in the first contingent and ended as a pilot.

Before he could locate him, Esther had wired through the Associated Press to locate Brand: Dean had been killed in action and was being flown home to Providence for burial.

As Press, despite difficulties of maximum security, Brand managed to get through in time for the funeral.

For a while he bore it stoically because Esther needed him. She was distraught, for the moment helpless before what was inconceivable to her.

He saw her through it, stayed at the house with her, though he was quiet, too quiet—almost mute—for the few days before Sylvia went to stay with Esther since he had to go back to Iraq. He wanted to. He had to get away. His silence was ominous. He was filled with seething, but as always when in tumult he held himself in and couldn't speak yet.

What smote him was the sight of Dean lying there. It struck all of us though we avoided talk of the resemblance: Dean was the spit and image of Brand's father.

Both boys were dark, skin and hair, as if *his* presence insisted in them.

The rest of us could talk of it after he'd gone, but Brand didn't let loose until long after the war when he learned that his son had been in a group killed by one of our own Patriot missiles.

"Missiles!" He lost himself in one of his increasingly frequent tirades. "Rockets and missiles and NASA and defense . . . missiles made by murderers. Yes, murderers—Hitler and the Germans with their V-1's and V-2's and the rocket team and my father. My father! *He* killed my son, but not just my father and not just the Germans and Saddam, *we* killed him, the Americans

71

and Bush and the Russians and the Japs and Roosevelt and
Stalin and Hitler and Mussolini and the Spaniards and Americans with their civil wars and the Huns and Persians and
Romans and Carthaginians and Greeks— It never stops, it's in
us, desire passion madness chaos. We kill our own. Yes, my
father killed his grandson. We all kill—because *madness*, do you
hear? Listen, Ferris— All wars are one vast motion in everything
that never stops, and earning the bread, and housework, the
kids conceal it, but if you look straight into the veil everything's
seething. We're monsters eating our own flesh."

So I understood why his terrible silence after his father's
death, his illness and retreat—he could *not* speak, he was living
in his father's house, he was living in the house of the man who
had already devoured a part of him, why he had had to escape
with me to Madrid.

Now from the grave his father, all his fathers, had devoured
another part of him, half of his own future, half of his infinitesimal immortality.

Would his father never stop devouring him?

It was then that he hated his father most: because *war*.

He hated Peenemünde—he couldn't forget he'd been con-
ceived there—hated the rocket team and Hitler and Huntsville
and his childhood and youth because of that talk that talk that
talk of Nazi, Nordic, Aryan—

*Remember when you came to Huntsville the first time after
graduation? It was all beautiful—wasn't it?—but beautifully
contrived*, Brand wrote sometime after the funeral. *That night you
saw my world. Their's was cut off for the evening. You saw nothing
of our real world.*

His father was wrong—Paul could write, especially under
impulse.

*Did you hear "Speak only German in this house?" No. And you
didn't hear the "cluster" speaking German and talking about
"their" eternal culture, "their" music, "their"—* He always wrote
their, it always defined his own stance—*words that were still
"their" lifeblood, that defined "them," "their" living past: Aryan*

Reich Jew Bloodbrotherhood Culture Deutschland über alles, against which he silently rebelled when he was old enough to realize *the wall* his father and a few cohorts had built before The Wall his father's nation would build to divide it, separating that everyday world they earned their bread in but hated and the Germany they carried that came alive when they were together. Their German circle was a contrast to the German community so adjusted and happy in that beautiful city in the Tennessee valley, for the German community had no such wall around them.

Brand rebelled by clinging to *his* language, English. Though he must speak Deutsch Deutsch Deutsch at all times at home and spoke it perfectly, he made his accent so perfectly American, so accent-free and colloquial, that anyone would doubt his German origin *of which otherwise he was proud.*

English became my side of the wall against my father's German, his ideas, and his closed society at home.

I remembered then his almost too perfect English at Bristol High and his "Brand here!" when Miss Bradford called his name on the class roll.

In high school most of the time I was on his side, antimilitary. We were both beyond the "playing war" stage, and neither sympathized with "the glamor of war," which some of our classmates exulted over. My father had been drafted close to the end of the war. He was a radio operator on a B-29 shot down over Germany. I was born after his death in 1945, so I never knew him. My mother went into the zipper factory in Warren, and days left me with my grandfather; together they did a valiant job of bringing me up. So though I could sympathize with Brand even in the early school days whenever he told me he was unhappy with his father, it was a limited sympathy because at his grandparents' I saw his world was nothing if not genuinely homey. And I could sympathize with the loss of his father somewhat because I had never known mine, though he could not have known the absence, the emptiness, the even strange blank, when other boys spoke of their fathers as pals, playing ball, taking trips, meeting on the dock or at the drugstore or the

5&10 or going to the circus on the Common, watching the Fourth of July parade or the regattas in the harbor. The only man in the immediate family, since my grandfather was not always with us, I soon became the head of the family: "Don't you think we should, Ferris?" "What would you do, son?" "We'll do whatever you think best."

After Brand's father died, and more frequently after Dean was killed in action, he would call and talk long, and at intervals he would suddenly appear in Madrid—the city was his lodestone:

"Because of Goya," he'd say. But, though I never said and he never said, I knew it was as much because *Bristol, home, father, son*. They were where I was. He could go to Providence to Esther and Rich, but they were *now*, without *him*; with me he could bring the earlier past to life. Between us was *then*, was his father; between us were silent *fathers*, his and mine and all our fathers, the world-savior-destroyers whom we hated with an indestructible love.

"And Carmen?"

"She helps." He laughed, because he was very **mimado** by Carmen; nobody had ever spoiled him as she did.

"Be careful, Carmen. The man has a habit of running off with my women."

"I couldn't have the first girl. In high school we were all in love with Clara. Sylvia was the result, a happy one, of circumstances. Three's the limit. I've given up the search."

Carmen went philosophical. "The victim can't help himself—the search doesn't give up the victim."

"And the Vietnamese girl?"

"You would bring her up," Brand said. "That girl was my teacher—and for a while my savior. What else? She was crucial. What she taught me—no, what she made me discover—was a wonder in the body. Until then . . ."

"The fruits of war. You see, nothing's purely negative—"

"You devil! You play with my deepest beliefs."

"No. That girl did. She made them broader, didn't she?"

He yielded, but hated to. "Infinitely—by narrowing them to one thing."

"Shall we leave the victim to his reveries?" Carmen smiled with that understanding Brand so loved in her.

In private I said to her, "He loves you too."

"Of course he does, but don't deceive yourself. What woman has ever given him friendship and tenderness and mothering without the least intimation of sex?"

"Oh, I don't deceive myself. Don't *you*. Even with mothers and sisters there's the least indication. I recognize Mother Earth when I see her."

"Trust her then." She kissed me.

"Infinitely," I said, "*sister*."

"Exactly," she said.

We laughed. She drew me down.

After the Gulf War, he didn't come home with the American yellow-ribbon, flag-waving euphoria over victory in the forty-three-day war. His photos said too much about the greed and meanness that led to hate and fear and sometimes to love and nobility, yet they were no match for the madness in his photos of the massacre of 450 unarmed men, women, and children, the entire village of My Lai, by U.S. troops in Vietnam. He was tired, not merely physically worn but emotionally stunned by the monsters war had aroused and revealed in allies and enemies alike. And despite the marvels of his photos, which so impressed his *Washington Post* editor that he would press him to gather them into the book that Harper's did, he felt he had failed. He knew he had.

"Something's evaded me, Ferris. Something keeps on evading me."

Ironically, that evasion brought out the fortress in him. He threw up protective walls to work behind.

We were back in his Providence apartment a couple of months after the war.

He was excited. There was that quick in him, the fast eye and rapid hand movements, and his rushes.

"I've gone back to working with faces."

"I thought you were exhausted."

"Who said I wasn't? But since when did that stop me? I thought all life was built on failures that goaded it on."

"So you're evolving?"

"If trial and error's the case."

"Is it?"

"Blunders!"

"Do I get to see some of the blunders?"

"Get to see! You've been a witness to my blunders since you've known me. And what blundering!" He burst into such bold laughter he finally had to wipe his eyes. "But look—I've been experimenting with photomontage—oh, the technique's old hat—but with . . . a vengeance?" He chortled. "Sit there." Before an easel.

"What's with the easel?"

"Handy. You'll see."

"*Jesus*!" The photographs were so enormous they almost intimidated. And when he turned them over, they did.

"Holygod!"

"Exactly!"

But I knew his control. He was seething.

At first sight the photo assaulted—an assemblage of mouths, vertical and horizontal eyes, segments of heads, fragmented profiles, ears of every size, some pressed against the viewer's eye, and tiny heads of every angle as if imbedded throughout the photo. Every bit of the canvas was covered—incomplete, it nonetheless bled off the canvas. But, magically, from a distance the solid-looking imbedded heads seemed to emerge from one enormous head as fine as a spider web, almost an illusion.

At first sight the chaos blinded. Then I saw.

"Why, it's Dean!"

"It's getting to be," he said.

The head was in a state of dissolution.

"Isn't it finished?"

"Oh, yes, but not complete. He's not. There's more to him than that."

He slid it off and one by one showed Dean and Dean—fragments of his face so arranged as to create Deans never seen before.

"A Medusa head," I said.

"This is the only way I can explore him."

He was not only effervescent; sharing it, he was actually giddy, excited as always when he had me under a spell.

"Explore him?"

"Yes." He broke out with his mother's favorite popular song from some musical: "'Getting to *know* you. Getting to know *all* abouuut you.'" And burst into biting laughter.

"Why do you see him that way?"

His head gave a quick jerk in my direction.

"Because he's my son!"

But I saw the question blunted. He lowered his eyes and stared at the floor as if I had tossed some object there he couldn't make out. I hadn't meant to.

Whatever briefly deviated him, instantly he was Brand again, pointing out how he hoped *Dean* worked, what impressions he hoped it conveyed.

Gathered together and centered by Dean's almost invisible head, the parts gave the illusion of a complex web emerging from a point deep within the skull, but the head itself was dissolving into an infinitude of isolated bits. It was dizzying: you were peering deep into that web. If the abyss and the parts were horrific, the web itself was beautiful. The web *was* the head. The web *was* the spider. I don't think then he realized how much cruelty he had revealed in the overall montage—in the repetitions of sharp eyeteeth, salivating devouring mouths, scattered squinting lids, fingers latched to the lips like claws. . . .

Perhaps my question had stirred some silt in him and roused a monster he'd been unaware had settled there. I say unaware because Brand had the true artist's impulse—he felt before he thought.

At the time the spring the Gulf War ended, Rich was visiting his grandmother in Huntsville. Since his father's death, Brand had been able to enjoy his mother's company. Mrs. Brand had been thrilled to have the boys back then, and both—half in love with their grandmother—spent as many holidays as they could with her. After Dean was killed in Iraq, she doubly doted on "my only grandson," who loved "*meine liebe Grossmutter*." In fact, Brand himself had succumbed to speaking German "at home," and the boys despite their bungling German insisted on speaking their grandmother's language. When they were leaving her house after their first visit since Mr. Brand's death, she gripped Brand's hand, he told me, and said, "This is the first day I truly feel at home in America." "Because nobody cares what language she speaks," Brand said, "nobody's listening, nobody's watching—any of us." But he said it sadly because he knew how his mother had loved his father and what it had cost them all to live with his presence.

So, perhaps in part to console Mrs. Brand for both his grandfather's and his brother's death (and surely to reach out in his loneliness for Dean since they were "more than brothers, intimate friends," Brand had said), Rich visited her often, especially on long vacations or when Esther was on trips out of Providence.

It was that Easter of '91, just after showing me the photomontages of Dean, when Brand went down to his mother's in Huntsville to take more photos of Rich to help him go on with his exploration of Dean—"getting to know *all* abouuut you," as Brand had so cryptically sung.

And it was on a day like any day in Huntsville around Easter time, mild, fragrant, sunny, with streets of dogwood blooming white as sunlit foam and the isolated redbuds covered with myriad tiny purply flames and the azalea tips waiting; it was on such a day, quiet as any day of vacation or routine, when the least gesture, habitual and necessary, seems insignificant and unrelated to anything as quiet and routine as the way to ruin or death or revelation, that Brand picked up the *Huntsville Times* and read of the boy who had been accused of killing his wife and one-year-old baby; and he chanced to see in the lower left-hand corner of the news photo a familiar face in the courtroom.

"Jerry Wicklow! He covered the Gulf War with me, for the *Trib*."

The next morning he was waiting with the crowd outside the courtroom. The case, as always with murder, was sensational, but this case triply so—a double murder, and the murder of a child, and that child the murderer's infant son.

"Jesus H! Paul Brand!" Jerry cried, and gripped. "Man, you're a sight for sore eyes."

And after an afternoon of Gulf War and photography and the murder case of Lester Galt over drinks at the Fogcutter, and not even at Jerry's insistence but at his own intrigue, roused as Jerry described the case, he decided then and there to make use of his Press pass.

So Brand saw the boy—he was just that, twenty-three—as the officers brought him in. He saw the boy enter and halt an instant. Brand was standing close by, facing the boy, and for a second they stared into each other's eyes. Actually it was Brand who stared at the boy. What impressed him was that the boy *was* staring, but not at anyone or anything in sight, it seemed. He was staring blankly at some no-man's-land straight ahead, where nothing was. He was staring absolutely without expression as if nothing either left or right of the aisle existed.

And I knew the instant Brand later said to me, "You should have seen the boy's face, Ferris," and described it, what had happened:

He was trapped.

By one of those peculiar recognitions that may lead to destruction, he was halted by that face.

But it was the why of the boy's terrible look—passivity? indifference? detachment? resignation?—which finally, yes, tortured Brand.

Because when he day after day had heard the case and knew the reported "facts" and the conflicting points of view and the reconstructions of the double murder, Brand said, "I can't understand the judge or lawyers or witnesses. As I see it, no-body is speaking the boy's language."

"His language?"

"Nobody seems willing to suspend judgment and imagine what he went through at the moment he committed the crime. His lawyer makes his case. He bases his case on the boy's first moments with him, because since then the boy hasn't talked. He won't talk. He said once and only once, 'I told you how it was. I can't change how it was.' He maintains his silence. What's so terrible is how outside the trial the boy is. He seems to *know*—to have known from the first moment—the end. He's so passive you'd think the trial's over and no one there knows it and he's simply enduring it for their sakes, for the process. Listen—"

I knew the case from the papers. Then I followed it with greater interest because Brand was there and related in more detail than the papers what was happening in the courtroom, but mostly because of the effect the case was having on him.

"Lester Galt is accused of having murdered his wife and infant son. His lawyer makes the case—it's the boy's, Ferris, it's what he's said to have blurted out in the first moment with his lawyer —that the boy is innocent and the wife guilty. The boy loved his wife too much ever to hurt her, the boy loved his son too much to hurt him. When he got home his wife was cooking supper (everything was still on the stove when the police arrived) and the son began to cry. The baby was in the bedroom, and she went in to settle him. He cried and cried till she shook him. Something must have happened to her because she wouldn't stop shaking the child and shouting at him to shut up so loud that Lester Galt rushed in. She was shaking the child *like a rattle*—the boy's words. He tried to take the child from her, but she paid no attention. He was afraid she'd kill it so he grabbed her. She wouldn't let go. He struggled, but couldn't stop her. He had her by the throat then. He said *he* couldn't let go he was so intent on saving the child. He wouldn't let go till she let go. He must have strangled her unintentionally. In the struggle they fell and she let go of the child. Quick he called 911. An ambulance and the police came in no time. He was sitting with the boy in his lap. She was still on the floor. The boy was dead. And the wife dead. That's the defendant's case. There was no motive for murder, no motive except the most unbelievable motive of all, murder for love—for love of his son —by a boy who loved his wife. Friends and neighbors testified to that, how much they were in love, how good he was to her, how good they were together. Accidental murder—for love. But it was the girl's family who had accused the boy of murder. They brought an arsenal of testimony against him—the boy's arguments with his wife, attacks, threats, making her so nervous she feared him, sometimes spent nights with her parents or escaped to relatives' houses. The prosecuting attorney's case you can imagine, you can lay it out easily: how the boy was already upset about his work, his job was on the hit list and, in the prosecutor's words, Galt wanted *out* of his responsibilities so feigned his fury over the late supper, triggered the child's screaming and his own frenzy, killed them both, strangled the boy and then the wife, and fabricated his story about killing his wife to save his child.

"And—this is what's so terrible—the boy won't speak, he's stubbornly and sullenly silent. His silence works against him more than anything. You'd think he *wants* to die—he wants to go *with* them, Ferris."

"Nobody wants to die, Brand."

"Don't be so sure of that. I'm not. Ferris, the boy *looks*— you'd swear he's staring into another world, seeing what we can't. He doesn't take his eyes off it."

Brand pinned himself to the trial. He suspended every activity while the trial went on, day and night ate, drank, breathed *trial*, *lived* at the courthouse through the slow weeks, the hung jury, awaiting the day-after-day deliberations, till finally some detail turned a juror and the count shifted—a verdict.

Guilty.

The verdict enraged Brand.

"Galt's guilty because he didn't talk. His silence condemned him. He was secret. They took his silence for guilt."

Sentenced to die in the electric chair.

"For murder, Ferris. *Two*. One murder he committed accidentally. It *had* to be. He couldn't, wouldn't, have lied about such a thing. And one murder he *couldn't* have committed except indirectly, by not letting go of the wife so that she squeezed harder, strangling the child, so he's made responsible for that death too. He was too innocent—I'll go down believing that. Call him stupid—but innocent too."

Guilty, but not.

Innocent, but not.

Guilty *and* innocent.

"The trial condemned the boy, but it resolved nothing, don't you see?" Brand said. "Stalemated. The issue's stalemated." Brand was too. "Because he unintentionally killed her to *save* his son. Which motive prevails? Here's a man caught between love and love. He tried to save them *both*, and in trying to save them both, he destroyed them both—and himself. He may even have *caused* her to strangle the child by trying to save him. But how could he have known? How separate one impulse from the other?"

As far as anyone knew, the boy spoke again only after the trial. Though the papers had reported the rumor earlier when it was thought a plea of temporary insanity might have gotten the boy off or gotten him a lighter sentence, in his cell the boy had said to his lawyer, "But I'm not crazy and I'm not sick. You know I'm not. *I* know I'm not."

"The boy wouldn't accept the lie. He wouldn't *let* the lawyer lie." Brand was frenetic. He pummeled the chair arms. "If the boy's story is true, he has every right to live. He has every right to live anyway, and *that's* the truth—yes, every right."

I had never seen Brand so close to losing control. I could swear he had tears in his eyes. He seemed even to lose his words, repeating ". . . every right . . . yes . . ."

After the trial his lawyer reported, doubtful to many, that in

a burst of passionate sincerity—eloquent, as the lawyer saw it—
Lester Galt said, "I told the truth. Why didn't they believe me?
I thought all I had to do was tell the truth and they'd believe
me and set me free. Don't they understand? I loved my wife. I
loved my son. Why would I kill them?"

From Brand's reaction, anyone would have thought Lester
was his son. Brand brooded—not for days, but weeks—after the
trial. Brand could have seen himself in that boy.

What I realized, looking back after his grandfather's tele-
gram, was that the boy was about his son's age.

But the case was not over for Brand.

He had a file of photos of the trial. I saw him seldom in the
months following the sentencing, but back in Madrid I had
fixed in mind the image of Brand in his studio in Providence
staring at those photos spread on the table, and I remembered
his description of the boy in court, staring, "seeing what we
couldn't."

I wouldn't have worried about Brand. I assumed there was
no need to worry, the boy having been sentenced, his case no
longer news, and time having absorbed that spectacular event
into the multitude of spectacular events that gradually diminish
to one more in the endless series of murders. No, there would
have been no need for worry—except that another chance event
kept Lester Galt alive in him.

Not long after Galt had been sentenced, a TV station in
California wanted to show *live* on a national network the electrocution of a condemned murderer. The case caused a national
polemic on TV and a rage of articles and essays in magazines
and in newspapers throughout the nation: What would this
ultimate horror, this private moment, this forbidden sight, this
invasion of life's most sacred event, do to the public? The answers ran a spectrum from an audience shocked to an audience
deadened by the spectacle of a man's death throes on television.

Long distance Brand said, "What it would do to the public
would eventually be nothing. The effect on the masses, as in the
case of all the quickies of the media, will run itself out in no

time and be as meaningless as Chappaquiddick. What's so terrible is what it would *not* do. Oh, it would satisfy their moral aim by showing the terrible end to a life of crime, *the* final moment of quiver and shudder and stillness—an awe in itself; but it wouldn't convey *who* that boy is."

"Who? He's—"

"*They*'re who he is, but that's they're last concern. Why don't they see how fragile the body is? But the motion in us is so strong, it doesn't want us. Electricity doesn't kill *it*—electricity takes life back into it. What is it, Ferris?"

The question was really a cry.

I thought, He's identified with that boy. He's *thinking* him.

"Televising the execution wouldn't alienate us from the horror, but from him, and that would alienate us from ourselves because he's what we're made of, and we don't know what that is."

Though there was no longer any reason for Brand's being in Alabama, for months before Galt was electrocuted he kept a close eye on the papers for news of the boy—any appeal, retrial, stay of execution, the chosen day. And when the date was announced, Mrs. Brand later told me, you could see the tension in Brand. Brand himself told me after his collapse how each day closer to the execution had made him imagine *hemmed in*, enclosed by cell walls, by the electrocution room walls, until he imagined his own skin walled him in—the pending execution, he said, excited something inside him that veered and leaped and struck against the walls to escape his body.

Galt's electrocution came at the very moment of the passionate controversy over televising the California execution live. The notoriety doubly roused the passion in Alabama over Lester Galt's electrocution and brought railing and rioting to Atmore. Days before the scheduled execution, crowds with placards picketed the prison: *An eye for an eye. Killing kids is cruel—this is not. Burn him.*

On Galt's final night, Brand waited with the crowd outside the prison at Atmore. They had given him license as Press to be at the electrocution, but he wouldn't go in, he refused to photograph those last moments.

"*I* couldn't. Would you violate yourself?" Brand asked me not long after. It was during his collapse, only a couple of weeks before his grandfather's phone call to me in Madrid to tell me he was dead, by his own hand. We were in his mother's house in Huntsville.

He took the execution as a personal onslaught climaxing months of apprehension about the boy's fate.

But that night he couldn't leave the prison. He had to be there. He had to know against all hope that the boy had been electrocuted.

"And I do know." He whispered it weak, almost voiceless, too devastated. "I do."

I waited.

I couldn't urge him—he was too lost in it. It would come.

It did.

"I waited outside the prison. There was quite a crowd because of the California TV business—and it *was* controversial, too controversial. People in both camps wouldn't let up—shouting, name-calling, right till the very last minute, midnight. Then just *before* came the cries It's time, Two minutes to go, one— Cries for. Shrieks against. And then—it was only a moment, a moment years long, if such a thing is possible, *you* know —the lights inside and outside the prison dimmed. The stillness was so sudden it terrified. Time itself died. They froze in that quiet. Then light came back strong. The crowd erupted. People shouted and screamed and laughed and cried. They were all motion. Their arms flagellated the air. In the dark the light struck those raised fists and faces. The faces glowed and the eyes glittered under the prison light. I couldn't tell who was *for* or *against*. All I could see was that rage of light in the faces, the eyes all the same. I turned the camera on the crowd. Like lightning I took photo after photo of those faces. I couldn't stop. I had to capture them before they broke up. I did. You'll see. Yes, you'll see them. I had the photos here. I had to see them. I couldn't believe that night. My mother took them. 'They're making you sick,' she said. 'Let Rich take them to Providence when he goes.' But I keep seeing those faces. They were filled. It was the light in all the eyes, like liquid. *That's* what I wanted to capture. I thought I did. But maybe I failed. . . . If nobody else sees it . . . ?"

"You saw it."

"Still, I couldn't shape it."

"But you saw it."

"Yes."

"You know."

"Something . . . ugly, beautiful . . ."

"You caught it."

"No. The camera did."

"But you—"

"The camera!"

"But you *know*."

"I didn't create it. It's raw. With no form. *My* eye saw it different, my imagination. I can't *do*, Ferris. My imagination rearranges, my hands ache to rearrange, but they can't . . . I have to hang onto the camera. I'll go under without it . . ."

"You must have captured something or you wouldn't be so attached to them."

"Something, yes. But I don't know what they're for. Yes, I do. They're for me. Because I don't know if anybody else'll see it. I caught it—maybe the camera *did* get what I saw? You'll see. Yes, you'll see them. And you'll tell me. You will. You won't lie, will you? You never did, Ferris."

Nothing, it seemed to me at the sight of him lying there weak, devastated, distraught, no, nothing had ever been so important to him.

"You know I will," I said.

But I didn't tell him. I would have if I'd seen the photos. I said good-bye to him. I didn't know it was the last time I would ever see him.

The second call was from Brand's grandfather too. He was tranquil this time, and I was, though as we talked—I asked about his wife and Esther and Rich and Brand's mother—there were those little intervals of silent emotion and most when finally he told me there was the sealed envelope Brand had left for me.

"For whenever you come home. He wanted you to have all his papers, everything."

"He said that?"

"*Ja*. It's in the will too."

There was a long stillness. Each mention must have made him relive the news of Brand's abrupt end.

What he'd left them.

"You'll be coming?"

"Yes."

"You have an idea when?"

"Soon."

"Good!" His voice pitched high.

"As soon as I can finish my manuscript."

"And you can stay with us." When he added, "*Willst du?*" for an instant I was the boy seventeen, not the man forty-seven.

He must have forgotten I had parents on Hope Street, just some blocks away from him. And maybe for one instant he forgot that I was not Brand.

When I replied, "*Nein. Mit meiner Mutter, Grossvater,*" a little laugh tore from him.

"*Ja.* But we will expect you."

"I'll be there *wann ich kann.*"

"*Wann du kanst.*" His voice resounded with genuine pleasure. "Oh, and grandmother says Come—*und schnell.*"

When he said good-bye, I wanted to cling to his voice. Cut off, I felt bereft of all the years, adrift and too far from what would not only never come again but drift further and further from me.

"You'll go with me?" I asked Carmen.

"No. You'll want to be alone there."

"Will I?"

But I knew she was right.

"Yes." And with her usual perception she said, "It will be a long journey, Ferris."

"Will it?"

"Longer than you think. But I'll be with you, both of you. You know that."

"Yes."

"Don't hurry," Carmen said. "Stay as long as you need to. And don't worry about me. Just keep calling."

She knew I was nervous, with that kind of strangely adventuresome anxiety that besieges because you have not buried your dead so they have not come to rest in you. But I wasn't going back to a ghost. I was going back to Brand. In my imagination he was in Bristol, where he'd wanted to be, but not in the cemetery. Since his grandfather had located me after the funeral, I had nothing to confirm his absence. He was still too alive to me. I was sure I'd find him on the streets in town, in the house, at Esther's, Sylvia's, his mother's. I had to see. I had to know.

By his own hand.

So, with my manuscript finally ready for the publisher, I flew Iberia to New York.

When I arrived, too tired to go to a hotel, too tired to sleep, after Customs I caught a taxi straight to the station and took the train to Providence. The trip is four hours. I'd still arrive before it was too late to call Esther or Sylvia. In a hotel I'd feel too alienated from home ground.

Goya, Are You With Me Now?

"Ferris!" Esther cried. "Where are you?"

"Downtown. At the railroad station."

"In Providence!"

"In Providence." I laughed. It seemed so unreal.

"Oh, I'm so relieved! How I've wanted to talk to you. You'll stay here, of course. Ralph's in Albuquerque." Ralph, I took it, was the new "constant." "Well, there's always plenty of room even when he's here. I'll be right down for you."

"Don't be silly. I'll take a taxi. It's raining like hell, and it'll be faster."

"Ferris! I can't believe it. Oh, I can't wait to see you. I'll whip up something. If I know anything, you haven't eaten a bite."

"Well . . ."

"I thought so! See you in a few minutes. And hurry."

Somewhere out there were Prospect Park, the School of Design, Brown, the harbor; but in the dark, the hard rain against the panes made the capitol dome and streetlights and building windows come in confused smears and glitters determined to blur memory.

Esther, always so calm, had said hurry. She was anxious to see me, of course—in a way, I brought Brand to her—but also to talk about Brand, surely because she knew *I* hadn't really been able to talk to anyone about him—and had she? After all, who'd had more contact with him over the years since his, and my, divorce than I'd had?

And she did talk. Once we'd hugged each other silently—she'd held me long with a kind of moan of relief, making me feel like a prodigal son returned—we stood looking at each other with an actual joy, a recognition of something solidly *home, past,* to cling to. She was two years older than we were, but that chiseled face was still beautiful, the hair drawn taut in an austere dark bun, even commanding on that swan neck, with a "sensual indifference" that had so captivated Brand. Once she'd gotten me comfortable in the den—it had been Brand's study during their marriage—and over a drink and then a TV tray of hot goulash—"Lucky you. Leftovers. One of my few

89

specialties. You always liked it"—sure then that I felt at home, out of the blue she talked. Actually we'd skirted talk of Brand as long as we could do so naturally, though she must have known why I'd come back.

At last she said, "Rich was devastated."

"I can imagine."

"It was Rich who found him."

"Rich!"

"You didn't know?"

"No. Brand's grandfather didn't give me the details."

"Well, that's understandable after what he's lost—there's only Rich now. But Rich won't talk about his father—the least mention and he goes silent and looks blank. He's holding it all in. It was horrible for him. He'd come home for a visit. His father hadn't been back long; he'd been recuperating in Huntsville at his mother's house after that trial he'd followed so closely—"

"I was there—after his collapse."

"He said. Well, he'd gone to Bristol when he was well enough. He'd spent so much time away all year that he'd decided to move back into his grandparents' house—it was a thrill for them, he said, and he was always happy there—so dropped his apartment but worked out of his studio of course. The work was piled up, he said. The trial had set him back. But people, so many famous people, had waited—he had work for a year. They came from everywhere to be photographed by him, he'd made such a reputation for himself. Well, you know all this . . ."

"Yes."

A gallery of his portraits would make a history of our time.

"But . . ." She stared, pained, down over the harbor. I thought she was about to break. After all, he was part of her mind and body and sons and days, and no woman can free herself—or, I suspect, fully wants to—from what helped make her what she is. She turned to me and said, her tone questioning, " . . . that wasn't enough . . ."

I shook my head, thinking *He wanted what you have*, and I

couldn't help thinking *Why?*, knowing he'd finally learned he had confused his love for Esther with his obsession with Esther's genius. He had preserved both till the very end. But he'd had his own vision, and he'd tried so hard to convey it not only in his photographs but in talk to me. Talk was difficult for him because he knew intuition had to be spoken to; intuition had to grasp it on sight without words. In fact, he was never jealous of Esther and her reputation, but he *was* jealous, in a protective sense, of her genius, proud to be close to it and share it in so far as he could. He was proud not with *vanity* but with true *pride*, *humble* pride before what was incredibly but humanly possible.

"But why wasn't it enough?"

"Because he had to depend on the camera. *He* wanted to do more than a camera can do."

"That's impossible."

"Exactly. He wanted to do the impossible, but—" A great sense of grief came over me at the thought of his years of obsessive struggling. I saw her lower her eyes. "—he couldn't."

"Why couldn't he accept—?"

I interrupted. "Who does? Which of us?"

She gazed at me. Her gaze struck bone. *You* I knew she was thinking.

"And how *could* he?" I cried. "He had vision, he had imagination, but they weren't enough. He had to depend on the camera. Without it he couldn't reveal what he'd perceived, but he couldn't with it either. He loved the camera but hated it. He wanted to be free of it, but was bound to it. He could do almost anything with it, but not enough. Yet he was helpless without it."

"How you understood him, Ferris."

"Not enough, but I'm trying."

"Had you been here, you might have—" She caught herself.

"No. Nobody could have saved him." I was startled by my own words. That seemed a raw truth I wouldn't have thought a moment before, but talk made it all too logical. "He might have gone mad otherwise."

"You really think that?"

H. E. Francis

"Yes. I'm surprised now he didn't. He'd learned his limits, but he wanted to break through them. *You* have. Painters have, but photographers never. The two arts are different, but he had a gnawing desire to go beyond the photo because his vision went beyond it, but his hand couldn't capture it. Yours probes. *He* wanted to do in his way what you do in yours. But there was always the camera, his wife the camera—it *was*—but a bad marriage, bad, it couldn't take him where he wanted to go."

"And *I* couldn't."

She rose and went to the wide window and stood looking down over the harbor, endless dark blurred by rain. At intervals the far lights shone sharp.

"But it was more, more. Whatever he wanted *was* his life. Without it he didn't want to live. It did cost his life. He was telling us something—or maybe telling just himself, resolving himself. And something—particular—drove him to it. Something singular, it had to be. And I'd like to know. I'd like to understand what he was going through at that moment. It would help. It would—"

"Don't torture yourself, Ferris. I know that's easy to say, but don't."

I gripped my drink and stared into it.

She came to me, bent over, and kissed the top of my head.

"Don't," she said. "You have to guard against that. I don't want to see you turn inward like Rich. He's locked into himself. He won't talk and nobody can talk to him about it. I don't know how long it will go on or what it'll take to make him reckon with it."

"Rich found him, you said."

She nodded. I knew she didn't want to tell me all. She wanted to shift the emotion away from me.

"Rich had gone to the studio that afternoon. He'd been used to calling the apartment, but since his father'd given it up, Rich had had to call him at the studio whenever he was visiting me. He'd called me the night before so knew his father was in town. His father virtually lived in the studio. He'd been going home

92

nights to his grandparents'. The next afternoon, Saturday—Rich had just come in on the train from New York, it was fourish—his father'd expected him so he went straight to the studio."

I knew the studio, of course—that frosted pane, the desk (Edna Ralston, the secretary's), shelves, cabinets, files, and the door to his two rooms beyond, two workrooms, one a kind of study. I could see it then.

"Saturdays the secretary wasn't there. The door was locked, but he could see him at his desk through the glazed pane. He knocked. His father didn't move or reply, and of course he was scared, and pounded—he still didn't move. So he broke the pane with his briefcase."

Esther hesitated. She knew I was seeing it. She would spare me, but couldn't.

"His father was sitting at his desk, dead. Rich knew at once, he said, though for a second he dared not move because in the half light there was a strange reflection over his father's face. Then he realized his face was covered with plastic. He had smothered himself."

"Smothered."

"Yes."

Brand! I saw him clearly, sitting there upright, enigmatic. I see his image now. A mask, but not. What he'd left us. But he couldn't have been thinking of us *then* . . .?

"Rich called the police, then called me. He hasn't said a word about his father since."

She sank onto the sofa, her hands lacing and unlacing over the folds of indigo blue that caught the light richly and made her hands white. They were long—they looked longer now, strong, like stripped fiber, almost masculine. Strangely, they made her body in that fluid indigo very feminine.

"But he must. He has to." She looked at me with straight appeal now, her eyes motionless, unblinking. "You'll talk to him. You'll go to him. You will, won't you, Ferris? If anybody can get him to, you can."

"You know I will."

93

"I know you will. You. You, Ferris. It's like . . ." Her hands groped. "It's like . . ." She lost her words. " . . . him . . . here . . . to have you."

I nodded.

Yes. Part of me was Brand sitting there. Part of me—or him—was for that interval restored.

Relieved, she rose, smiling almost to herself. "I'll fix you another drink. Then I'll show you my new work."

She seemed the Esther of old. Her abrupt buoyance was perhaps an escape to restore us too to our old bond, not merely to the old marriage days, but in a way to our own personal and somehow more intimate bond, more intimate because her work was our communion, art our mutual sustenance. If she had vision, I had insight. What she did, I articulated. It made us a pair that complemented the life she'd had with Brand. If Brand hadn't articulated what he'd seen in her work, his silence was an eloquent homage to it: her vision had stunned him, her execution baffled. If he had basked in her genius, he had burned too—and deeply. It had challenged all his invention with the camera. Her painting had been the first to make him aware of the vast gulf between her art world and his photography. And it had made him aware of the gulf too between his own vision and its realization, between his perception and his capabilities. He had wanted to paint. He had wanted to turn the camera into a brush.

"And I failed," he'd told me in Huntsville. He'd been talking about the execution photographs. I hadn't been able to judge because I hadn't seen them.

I saw him—I see him now—recuperating at his mother's, worn, not merely from that trial he'd followed, but from the long pursuit to capture something concrete that he'd seen *in* things, in everything, and from something he'd carried that had harried him, an undescribed, perhaps indescribable, impulse that had driven him.

In a way, I thought then, following Esther into her studio, he *had* drowned; in a way I had left him to drown. Had I—or anyone—been with him, would it have kept him from it?

I was thinking of our last conversation in Huntsville when Esther put the light on and her sudden realm materialized, thrusting the city beyond its spacious windows back into dark and rain. And if I'd had any illusion that I could have escaped thoughts of Brand by viewing her work, the instant I saw the canvases propped against the rear wall, for perspective no doubt, and the enormous canvas set on two easels, that illusion vanished.

They were rocks, ravines, walls.

"I'm deeper into stone."

Her hand rose and almost touched the edge of stone. She had painted the pivotal point where the walls of a divide met. It was stone but not cold, hard but not hard. They appeared warm, in browns, thins of ocher, spreads of beige, depending on the density, darker the closer to the meeting point.

"It looks alive!" I wanted to touch it. The rock looked deep. "You've taken us into it."

She gazed at it, serious, silent.

The more I stared, the more alive the stone seemed.

If only Brand—! I thought of his yearning, and the joy-agony it must have been for him to be so close to Esther, to love, lie with, and breed with Esther and yet stand alone, far from what was under the skin he touched, that mystery. He had gone into it, but could not hold it up to us.

"But how do you see—?" I prodded.

She laughed. "You with your eternal *How?*"

"It's my job."

"Yes."

But of course there was no *How?* that she could discuss. Any attempt would degenerate—and did—to a discussion of technique, not perception.

But I wanted that. I didn't want to leave. As long as we were talking, somehow the *other* was warded off, Brand's suicide seemed not to have happened, and I postponed my dreads. Brand. He wanted to know, but feared knowing.

"The stone insisted on its own recognition," she said.

It was her way of saying she intuited technique in the act of "feeling her way into stone."

She had gone from her last reductionist technique to an arrangement of striations composed of varying densities of light achieved surely through layers of infinitesimal hairlike lines coated over and then repeated and coated over and repeated."

She had found the flesh of stone.

"I'd swear the stone was alive," I said.

"Isn't it?"

She was not being coy or cryptic.

It was that perception which had made her one with Brand, and her ability to capture its implications in paint which had separated them. He couldn't survive living so near the flame he desired but was denied him.

"Yes." For the texture was as rich as skin, and warm; and the perspective lured the eye to that point of fusion. The stone suggested a throat, a far fusion of waters, a vagina, a rush through walls of space to a black hole; yet it was clearly stone.

I touched it.

There was a surface roughness.

"It feels gritty. You've ground something into the oils or the coating—pulverized stone itself?"

She smiled, a Mona Lisa teasing.

"Trade secrets of your universe?"

"Nothing of the kind. I'll demonstrate my alchemy for you next time you come. But—" Her face, and her voice, turned suddenly apprehensive. "—you *will* keep coming?"

I caught her fear, or realization. With Brand gone our world had shifted. The ground had quietly tremored and fractured all our lives. That moment was the first evidence of it.

"You know I will," I said, instantly realizing it was a half-lie. Already I felt adrift and knew the rift would widen since half the reason for our coming together had died. Brand was gone, memory of him would diminish, but there was still her art.

"You can't go to Bristol this late. You'll spend the night?"

"I thought I'd sponge—"

"Then why not a few days—at least the weekend? You'll have to be here a while this time, won't you?"

She was pleading for Brand's presence, as if she too didn't fully believe he'd gone, though my coming verified it. And when I had to leave for Madrid again, in a way Brand would go too, though he would always be latently present in Rich.

"The weekend, yes."

"Ohhh, Ferris—" She sighed with great relief and sank onto the sofa. "Then I'll call Rich. You can talk to Rich. You will, won't you, Ferris? He has no one to talk to since Dean. He trusted Dean so."

I realized then how crucial Rich's problem was. Esther, as sentient as she was, was not given to the least flagrant emotion; but her eyes filled now—surely from the confusion of the loss of Brand, her pleasure at seeing me, and this momentary relief over Rich—but fleetingly. She shook her head, rose, and said, "I need a nightcap. Don't you?"

Relaxed there on the cold blue sofa, she talked, meandering the way she would, her mind always following bits and tags in what seemed a careless associational chain but with that relentless logic of emotion. Perhaps impelled by the drink, the third, she wandered through her adventures since I'd seen her last: shows at Aspen and Caracas, Caracas both a personal disaster and a salvation. She had been mugged, but Ralph had rescued her. Ralph was a lawyer working on a case involving an international oil cartel. ("Coincidentally he knew my own lawyer, Brick, who'd seen me through the business of the boys' change of name.") Once back in the States, he had called from New York, come for a weekend, they had gone to that little place downtown, "You know, the French place everyone goes to for its onion soup." She laughed. "They have an enormous reproduction of my painting of the onion on one of the walls," a color reproduction taken at her first Aspen exhibit—"what? twenty years ago? You remember it. Brand had insisted on doing the photos for the Macmillan book, and where better than at the exhibit, where he had proper space and light."

Brand.

Strangely, neither had spoken his name till now. She was, I thought, maintaining control, distance, with "his father," "Rich's father," "he," "him." And at her own utterance now she halted as if, I thought later, she had at last reached and realized she had reached the threshold of a moment of self-purging, a kind of confession, because she went on then, unable to cease. All she'd needed, and was aware of it, was the mere relaxedness of that third drink in order to *say*.

"The art exhibits excited him. He was somehow happy, happiest even, when he was making those marvelous photos of my paintings. He would study them by the hour like the real paintings. They gave him a certain peace, a relative peace, at least for a while. I say that because always there came a point when that peace would turn to dissatisfaction, even sometimes downright misery. I want to say he thought too much about his photos—he *did*—but it was more than thinking. I believe he was certain that if he felt deeply enough he could do something original. The irony is that he felt even more deeply than he must have known. Maybe he couldn't finally contend with such profound depths of feeling, no matter what he blamed for rousing him. He did blame other things, oh never directly. I had to presume how much the least casual mention of father or mother or German or Jew stirred him up. His grandparents, so serene and reasonable and comfortable, were a wonderful contrast to his father; and even the contrast intensified his tensions with his father. Despite his love—and how deep that love was—for his mother, his unfortunate ally against the man she loved so passionately, even adored, Brand would say, . . . despite that love she too was an unconscious antagonist because her very existence kept him aware of that division. She might just as well have said, *Despite my love for you, my love for your father is stronger, and I could never go against him no matter what.* Naturally she'd never have said that. And not speaking must have been, partly at least, something of the terror—yes, terror—of Brand's growing up between them in a household where nothing direct could ever be said, everything was suppressed. For his father the war had never ended; in some continued fantasy in his head Germany hadn't lost and would be redeemed. They were on alien ground here. But it was *not* alien ground to Brand; it was *his* ground, his country. And his mother was caught in the no-man's land between husband and son, torn every minute of her life, so she could be fully the wife or the mother. Can you realize the hell her life must have been? Oh, it's easy, too easy, to think Leave, separate, divorce him, go back to Germany, go into exile elsewhere—all impossible. She's a woman of an old world with all the taboos, who'd never dream of such escape or salvation for herself or be sure of them for her son. Can you imagine the atmosphere Brand grew up in? Oh, again, it's easy to think *normal*, and anyone seeing that attractive, tall, handsome young boy with the all-American look would surely never imagine *pressure, discontent, misery*, even intense *self-consciousness*, except maybe—and then only after being with him enough—those outbreaks of skin at moments of extreme nervous tension. When I was married to him I didn't suspect their seriousness until those blemishes returned—he was so quiet about them, and about his ambition too, which I had no idea would lead to such nightmares. He had none at the beginning of our marriage. No, of course he didn't, or he was silent about them. It was surely our marriage that brought them out. I'd like to say if I hadn't married him, his problems would never have emerged, but I believe that'd be a lie. In time they'd have come out with someone else. And who knows what effect some other woman would've had on his work, or he on hers, for that matter. I've thought and thought about what was in him. What was it, Ferris? Was it born there? Was it impressed on him? Was it nurtured by that obsessed father and that obsessed mother? And did *I* bring it to a head simply by marrying him? Could I help it if he wanted an artist? I don't think he knew that. Perhaps he didn't *want* one. Perhaps if he'd known that, he'd have run from me, but everything in him was attracted to that. He couldn't have known what would happen when he approached me in the gallery in Huntsville. He was so personal and I was flattered, though that wouldn't have been enough if the man in him hadn't shown himself all push and go. I was lured—seduced—and me no innocent. He was so *sure* of himself, sure he wanted me, only me. He'd never wanted anything so badly; he wouldn't settle for anything else. Of course, he was young—we were—but he was so straight, candid, almost nakedly honest; yet there were things, I soon found out, he couldn't say—strange, because when he'd mulled enough he could command language. He was like you in that. But you know that."

"Yes. But I didn't have his vision. I don't."

"But he couldn't describe it."

"No, not any of his deep emotions."

"That's why photography was so important to him—it was concrete. Photos spoke for him. They said at a glance more than he ever could, or would."

"He was too silent. He had too much locked up in him. It took me years—years, yes—to . . . unravel some of his complexities . . . and he's still an enigma. Oh, at first, early in the game—game, yes, because from the beginning it was play, if serious play, and it became a serious challenge—more than anything he wanted to satisfy me, as a man, I mean. He was passionate because he was young; and he was an adventure, every man is. Brand wasn't merely passionate, he was desperate, though I was slow to realize it was desperation—because he was driven, and for a long time it was like being delirious to be on the receiving end of frenzy, madness—what else can I call it? Perhaps—precisely because of the pleasure—I was blind too long to the fact that he was alone—I don't mean he wasn't with me or that he didn't love me, but that he was alone in that frenzy. He was on a journey— You see? I can't say it any more than he could. He was trying to get somewhere."

"Get somewhere."

That was no surprise to me, though Brand, of course, would never have discussed sex with me, sex with Esther. He had too much intrinsic respect for his relations with all of us. Besides, he expected me to understand. He was always so *sure* I did, so he never had to speak, or why had we been almost blood brothers from the beginning? Now what surprised was Esther's probing. Once started, she didn't stop. The surprise to me was to catch a rare glimpse of her concentration to the point of passion, the passion that must have gone into those magnificent paintings. In fact, it might have been her ability to release that passion day after day into her paintings that accounted for her almost mystifying placidity. Her customary ease was an attraction and a comfort to anyone who came near her.

"Get somewhere, yes. He was using me."

"Using you!"

"My body. I mean I realized I was alone, and that might have been the worst shock—the revelation was—but not when I was honest with myself and faced the fact—and I was sure of it at that moment—that what must have attracted Brand in the first place and what usually attracted men to me was my indifference: and if I *hadn't* confessed that to myself I'd have hated Brand. I'd have said that he was using my body—he *was*, but he didn't know that. He'd have been shocked if I'd accused him of that. But *I* could have said I was using him too—I was, or my body was. You don't formulate such thoughts until after; you aren't aware of them till after, in my case after the divorce. Now things stand like obstacles; you have to confront them. Yes, my body used him. If I was indifferent in some ways, it's my nature, sex makes me a live object to myself, it makes me closer to things, it brings them to me, it—what?—opens up trees, flowers, stones, stars. I feel them. I could be, it makes me, one of them, or them me. And it isn't a frenzy to be released to something, or escape, or . . . whatever it was to Brand. Sensing my feeling must have hurt him. I—it's hideous to say, it hurts me to think it—I came to pity him. Yes, pity. And that was bad, it *was*, because my pity began to set him a little apart—I didn't want that, but you don't dictate feelings. It nearly broke my heart to see how he struggled for what I could never give him. The divorce hurt, but living with his silent suffering hurt more. I couldn't find a way to help him. And living with me agitated his dilemma—that was the only lament I ever had about my own struggles, happy struggles, with my painting."

"But they fed *him* too. Nothing pleased him more than to see you capture your vision time after time—that was almost incredible to him—but at the same time your achievement divided him. It constantly goaded him to achieve and reminded him that he'd failed—"

"But did he?"

Coming from her, the question startled.

She smiled that cryptic.

"You said he had vision."

"He did."

"Then he must have communicated it to you. He trusted you, Ferris. You were the only one Brand would really open up to. He seldom talked to me about that side of his work."

"Maybe he didn't want to hurt you."

"Maybe. But my point is—if he had vision, he hasn't failed if you've seen it."

"But I haven't."

"But you know."

I felt haunted. I'd had this conversation before. She was uttering his words.

I said, "He sometimes explained what he'd wanted to capture in a photograph. *He* saw it, he wanted me to see it, he wanted anyone who looked at the photo to see it. What he saw may even have been in the photo, but what he saw simply disappeared into the photo because he couldn't make it the primary focus. *He* knew that. He couldn't arrange—rearrange—what the camera caught. His imagination transformed what he saw, but of course the camera simply recorded whatever he turned it on. He could give it his angle of vision, but it stopped there."

"But he didn't. He kept at it, Ferris. And his struggle—he was always so silent—came to be terrible for me. You can imagine . . . day after day he'd stare at my paintings, he'd stare as still as a dead man. Did he expect to osmose something from them or be absorbed into them? Sometimes when he looked at me I began to feel he was accusing me—he *wasn't*—for not helping him. Of *course* he never thought such a thing. No question of that. He always turned on himself. He was like a man who'd never stop trying to climb out of a hole so deep there was no way out. And I was aware of how walled in he was. I must have been relieved to escape that when we were divorced. At the time any concern for him was buried among so many other personal considerations. I was aware of his obsession whenever he came back—*he* had no intention of escaping, he almost never missed an exhibition of my new work, and he was still in my life mostly because of the boys and sometimes you or Sylvia or his grandparents. Oh, I don't underplay his coming back for my work, but it didn't strike me with such force, never, until his grandfather called me to tell me. . . . Then. Yes, it struck me then that I had my part in his suicide. I was as guilty as . . . anyone else."

"But you couldn't have helped him either."

"Not helped avoid—?"

"No, nobody could have given him what God or chance had failed to give him. He could thank whatever for giving him talent and curse it for not giving him enough."

"And for giving me too much? Don't you think I felt that— call it injustice—more and more over the years?"

"You're not responsible for that. Nobody is."

"Ah, Ferris, don't try to soften edges. That's not like you. You're wrong. I'm responsible first to what's in me. No, I'm not responsible for what he had, but I am for some part of who he was and what he did."

"You couldn't have changed that either. He was Brand. He stayed Brand. He died Brand."

"He didn't have to die that way!"

I stared at her. *But he did*, I thought. No, I didn't *think* that. It came like revelation. It dazed. I went on staring at her face wrought with the pain of guilt. I'd have given anything to give her the answer which would, if not release her from responsibility, alleviate her guilt—because she *was* suffering. You don't get into a man's mind heart body the way she had with Brand and not feel that a part of you has died without the body grieving for what's lost. Then I *was* thinking it, *He did have to,* because if Brand hadn't . . . he *must* have imagined a long life of . . . a living death—it would be that, wouldn't it? He would go at it year after year being married to the camera, trying to make it do his bidding, trying to give it life as though if he kept insisting with faith and fidelity it would eventually be not merely an artificial mechanical extension of his arm but at last become his true eye and achieve the miracle of revealing the world of his imagination in images.

I lowered my eyes. I stared at the floor, at the grain in the old wide red pine. I said nothing.

"You won't give me any relief?"

Brand didn't have any.

But if I'd uttered that thought, it would have crucified.

"You'd make a good priest, Ferris."

I looked up, questioning.

"They don't speak, the priests. They let you. They answer with silence and turn the responsibility back on you. How many *Hail, Marys,* Ferris?"

She was only half jesting. Her tone, if it bit, ate at herself.

"If I were a priest . . ."

"You are. You're mine. I couldn't talk to anyone else about Brand, no one, not even Rich, especially not Rich. Despite Brand's travels, Rich was close to his father, very close. So who else to confess to?"

"Confess? But why? I can't give you—"

"Absolution? It's not what I want."

"Why confess at all then?"

"To unburden myself. I'll be rid of it then—part. It won't gnaw at me every day, it hasn't, but I had to say it, to know I'd said it—and to you."

"Why me?"

"To lay it on your shoulders."

She gazed hard at me, and long. I waited. I wouldn't ask.

Because she would say.

She did.

"It's why you came. I knew you'd come. I was waiting."

And as she said it, I realized there was a certain truth to it, or why had I called her first—merely because of the weather? or because of a quick place to stay? or because it was the most natural thing to do? She might just as well have said, "Because you *knew* I was waiting, and you'd want to know what I could tell you."

She might have called *me*. And I had the sudden fleeting thought that they were all waiting, caught in an unconscious movement to plant it on my shoulders, knowing that even without them I would assume it. Or why would his grandfather have called, and Esther be waiting, and Rich hoarding his story in silence surely for me, and Sylvia, and his mother, and . . . perhaps in some final way Brand himself? How was I to know? Already I seemed to have been the protagonist of a subconscious design, a design taking shape as each event became the emotionally logical cause of the next. I imagined Esther knew she was playing a part, but only realized it *now* as she motivated —at first simply by unconscious repetition and then by consciously instigating—my next move.

"You'll want to talk to Rich. He's in Huntsville with his grandmother. They're terribly fond of each other. He suffered, really suffered, in the years when his grandfather was alive because he couldn't see her—she wouldn't *violate* her word, never crossed her husband by visiting us as long as he was alive; but after his death Rich went, he went right away, and ever since, twice as often since Dean was killed. That was Rich's terrible moment—worse when he found out Dean was killed by our own troops. That turned Rich sour. He's bitter. It transformed his thinking about justice and made him see things as demonstrations of 'fickle fate.' Besides, his grandmother needed him. She had had really no one but her husband all the years since he'd disowned the boys, and when Rich rushed to her, she seized on him—he was not only a confirmation of the old man's presence, he was a liberation from his rigidity. That might have been cause for worry, but Rich was also looking for more than relief, he wanted the kind of knowledge of his father that only she had if she'd give it. And why wouldn't she? She couldn't hurt her husband or her son now, and she could help Rich immensely—and herself. He was a godsend—they *are* to each other."

Esther did not stop there. She had me then—and knew she had me, not merely because of helping Rich, though that was her preoccupation. She knew I'd answer her appeal for his sake as well as hers and, above all, Brand's. She knew that when she said Rich was looking for the kind of knowledge of his father that only Mrs. Brand could give. She baited me. She couldn't have known I had every intention of visiting Mrs. Brand though I wouldn't have gone directly to Huntsville if Esther hadn't with her sense of emergency reinforced my own desire to go, for there was nothing I wanted more than to know all I could about Brand. I wouldn't rest—and she knew I couldn't—until I had explained Brand's life to myself as completely as I could. Without that knowledge, I knew a part of my own life would be missing. Part? How explain part without the whole? No, in a real sense, my life depended on it, though the *why* of that I didn't know at that moment. Perhaps along with my deep friendship, that ignorance was precisely what impelled me.

So yes, I said, I'd see Rich first. I would postpone my visit to Bristol, to the Stockmanns and my parents. Actually there was no need for hurry. Mr. Stockmann had said "whenever you return." And the task surely would take some time—there would be Brand's papers to go through and whatever possessions he had left me.

"But you'll stay here as long as you like," Esther said, "at least to rest up a day or two." Ralph, her live-in, wouldn't be back for two weeks, though his returning with me there was hardly a problem. "And don't think you'll be interfering with my work. Why would I work with you here?"

That was not what I was thinking. My stay would give me time—she hadn't had any need to mention her—for Sylvia.

So I said, "Yes. I want to visit Sylvia."

I said *visit* diplomatically—I'd wanted to talk to Sylvia in private—so Esther didn't suggest inviting her.

The next day when I called Sylvia for dinner out, she suggested, better, an afternoon drive and then drinks at a hotel downtown. That would divorce us from any too familiar atmosphere. Neither of us wanted the obvious intimacy of places associated with Brand if we were going to talk with any objectivity at all—if we could—ironically *because* we did want the intimacy, but the emotion might blind us momentarily, for in her own way she too had loved Brand.

Her emotion was evident when she gripped me and kissed, and clung. I couldn't help feeling she was holding Brand in me, the foursome we'd once been, and then the four of us "redesigned" when Brand had sought consolation (or what?) in her.

"Consolation, no," she said, and smiled. She parked, but we didn't go into the hotel. "More like confirmation."

She backed the car out and drove out into the countryside out Pawtucket way. She'd changed her mind about the intimacy. She'd decided she wanted it. She was taking me to a small restaurant she and Brand had frequented "some good time after he'd divorced Esther" and was floundering. He'd never been a womanizer, but it was when he was—she laughed softly—"what? trying them out for size? I say that since what was missing in the women he'd dated before me was talk, not chitchat—movies, hairstyles, pop stuff, lifestyles—though Brand was interested in anything that revealed a person's character, the photographer in him no doubt. He wanted something more intimate. I shudder to say so because he didn't find it in me. He thought he was on the right track, but I could go just so far with him. That was no deception on my part. I genuinely tried. I thought with his help we could become what he needed us to become, a fairly complete pair. I wanted to give him a serenity he'd had at only brief intervals, all too brief, in his life with Esther—when each of the boys was born, with his first book of photos, sometimes in sex, or afterwards when sex so excited him (oh, he could *go on*) he was convinced he could *create*. Sex fed creation, he said. Oh, Ferris, you should have experienced him at such times, but of course you couldn't—no man can unless he experiences the woman's feelings—or you'd know how he suffered *after*, when he couldn't reach those heights in his work."

"But I can understand. I did. Do."

"Of course you do—if only from sympathy. I'm being egotistical. Perhaps what I'm saying would help you understand."

"Me?"

"Yes, you."

Again I had that peculiar sensation of an unconscious plan among them as if I were in a network of all their thoughts after Brand's death and they were waiting for me so that they could not only, as Esther had said, unburden it on my shoulders but also see what I would do with what they gave me. Maybe like me each wanted to know how she figured in the mystery of Brand. Yes, I had that intuition, not that they would live with that expectation, but that they would not be at all surprised if I did something that would return to them what they'd given me as part in some whole I might render up as if the very rendering— perhaps this was the key—were a collusive act of silence. And at that instant it struck me too that they had observed me over the years more closely than I had ever imagined and that each of them knew, in her own way, in her own experience with me, facets of me which I myself was only half aware of.

"I'd say it helped him that I wasn't any kind of artist. That was my greatest advantage with Brand. He didn't have to live in my shadow. In this sense, at the time, *you* wouldn't have done either because you're a critic and your eye never rests; his work would always come under your scrutiny, no matter how generous your friendship was, though he valued—infinitely—your cold eye and your sense of raw truth as you saw it."

"Brand said that?"

"Oh, yes, often. His respect for you—apart from your being his best friend—knew no bounds. Your approval meant everything to him—you have such high standards, as high in your field as he in his. You were something to match. You were a measure of his own success or failure. It wasn't that he had no confidence, though it sounds like that, but as a photographer—he was certain of his capabilities there—he—it sounds strange to say it—didn't believe in limitations. He wanted to, it would have made his life more comfortable, and who doesn't want to be at peace with himself."

I saw him then—I see him now—a lone figure in the fog.

"For two years almost, we made a success of it, and I don't mean merely sexually, though we had achieved some balance, because he came to me also as a friend. He could tell me anything—he didn't, I suppose no one does—but I can't tell you how endlessly he talked. He never did with Esther, at least not about himself, he said. Therapeutic—it *was*—but not enough."

She pondered as she poked her fork into the onion pie.

"This was his favorite dish here," she said. "Every once in a while he'd say, 'Let's drop in for onion pie.'"

"Yes. His grandmother'd make it. He'd ask her to. She loved spoiling him."

"Ahhh."

Wherever reverie took her, she was smiling. I waited, but she was silent too long.

I said, "What made you aware of that?"

"Of what?"

"That it wasn't therapeutic enough."

"I'm sorry." But she laughed. "I was remembering the night I made the pie myself. I tried to match this. An awful flop. We took one taste, looked at each other, and laughed like crazy, couldn't stop—like kids. I don't have the touch. I never tried again. I was trying too hard to spoil him, to fill some gap, make up for what was happening."

"What was?"

"I'd failed him."

"But you can't count that flop as failing him."

"No, no. I mention the pie simply because it was such an

explicit failure. I consider it the beginning. It spoke volumes. I knew I'd failed when he'd started to have nightmares."

"Nightmares?"

"All our talks hadn't helped him. Something he wasn't telling me. I'd touch him to wake him, ask if he was having a bad night. I'd take him in my arms to console him, the nearest I ever came to mothering him. 'I had a nightmare.' He never described them or even remotely suggested what they were about and I wouldn't probe. If he'd offered— But no one has a right to your dreams. Some people don't want to pursue them, want *no* right to them. The one thing *he* said that suggested how awful they must have been was 'They're not *my* nightmares. They don't belong to me. They belong to someone else. They must come from too far. I don't want them, but they got into my head. They're there now, and they don't leave. I'm responsible for them. But how did they get in me?' That haunted him more and more, but he wouldn't go on his own for any kind of relief, and I didn't suggest it. He worked so hard I was sure work would drive them out, but I was wrong. They came to interrupt and displace things. I'd see less of him. He'd spend more time with Dean and Rich. He'd visit Esther. He'd swim. You remember how he loved your mother's house in Greenport because of the Sound—he couldn't stay out of the water. Neither could you. You two would leave Esther and me on the beach. Thanks to those long sessions we became friends, such good friends, so that when he was gone, I had Esther. In a strange way, we both still had him and shared him. He'd never really left us. He'd visit the boys—and later they'd visit him for short vacations whenever he was abroad and where he could find a little time to tour with one of them."

I saw the figure then.

I was sure.

His father.

Or what his father had left in him.

I can hear now, as I heard at her mention of his nightmares then—I hadn't thought of it in years—the first time Brand had told me he'd had a nightmare. In the sixties—he'd come back from Vietnam—we'd had drinks at his place in Providence. That night the film *The Diary of Anne Frank* was on TV. I had wanted to see it. He was tired, but he was soon caught up in it. The history of that Jewish family with their friends hiding from the SS troops in a Berlin attic for over two years (futilely, as we learn from the diary discovered long after) must have clung to his mind as inseparably as smoke coating a ceiling because one night, years after, we spent a good bit of time talking about our remembered reactions. He confessed that for weeks afterward he dreaded sleep because the film had given him nightmares of associated guilt.

It was one of those moments that illustrate the typically clear logic with which Brand could analyze an experience that had earlier triggered something in him too deep for speech. We were speculating on possible reactions to the film.

"In time, we're removed from that event by more than twenty-five years. As gentiles I don't think we can feel what any Jews seeing it may feel. First, those Jews who actually lived through the experience must feel it unbearably, to the point of silence. Then those Jews who escaped but lost relatives butchered, gassed. Then all those Jews who served in the armed forces and those who didn't and whose families were not directly involved. Then, in time, the children of those lost and of those who survived, who were not witnesses but who had contact with witnesses, Jews and non-Jews; those who would initiate societies, organizations, write on the cause; and those of the next generation indignant from sheer daily association with family memory and talk and synagogue and cult and culture, sheer repetition by those who must and can't help but keep the Holocaust alive, like those writers of deep feeling and thought who will never, should never, let up. And there is a similar hierarchy of feeling, as time passes, in non-Jews who were in the war and close to the experience or not in the war but alive to it, those of the next generation whose connections with the earlier kept it alive, and those—whoever—of deep sensibilites who can

imagine from the facts, who one day far from the events will
record that horror, keep recording it, out of sheer reverberation
of agony—I won't say 'race memory' because that memory has
never kept us from killing one another before, but from the
passion itself that any history or story may impress on any sensitive soul."

Yes, I did have my convictions about his nightmares. I didn't
say so to Sylvia. I don't know why, though I said *Not yet* to
myself, *there'll come a day to tell her.*

Whether her intention or not, Sylvia had given me what she
could—the persistence of the nightmares.

"Despite the boys, the trial, and so much work and exercise,
the swimming, the nightmares didn't stop. If anything, though
not so frequent, they were deeper. He did say, 'They're harder to
get rid of.' And yet what I *was* curious about—what was curious
—was his abstract look. You know how one can stare *into* something in plain day which isn't there for you, but holds *him* with
such perverse fascination that *you* believe he sees something real
—he *does*—and since *you* know it's real to *him* you're led to
wonder what perversity controls us at such instances. Why do I
say perversity when nightmares are perfectly natural?"

"Natural, of course. What disturbs isn't the dreaming or even
the frequency, but the extremes in them that make the nightmares seem perverse."

"Except that his took him from me."

"You give them such power?"

"Yes, but you'd have to live with him to know. His habits
changed. Something was happening in his head. I'm sure it
was."

"Why do you say that?"

"I told you—I stopped being important to him. Oh, he came
home, he ate, we talked. At first he talked from—I believe he
began to feel—a sense of obligation. *You* know that's sooner or
later evident, and it hurts—but he couldn't help that. Out of
fairness, though it was hard—after all, I have an ego too—I
came to understand that he wasn't to blame. He was a victim of

himself—and, what's more, of his family and work and perhaps because of them his ambition. I knew—it was decisive—I'd failed with him, failed as a woman to fulfill him, though we'd begun well—sensationally, in fact—but that too, for him, I see now, was an escape—though I didn't know, I may never, what from. I knew I'd failed because he'd stopped coming to me— the sex stopped, almost abruptly—even as a friend. The night-mares were the obstacle. They were stronger than I was. They took his mind, then his body from me."

"Didn't you—"

"Oh, don't ask it. I had to come to that—*I* talked and talked. Suggested. And he listened—always with that sense of other-ness in his eyes. Occasionally he'd nod. I'd think *This* time he's actually paying attention, he *will* get relief, professional help. He *wants* to be free of the nightmares. But you know, Ferris, I came to believe he wanted those nightmares."

"Nobody wants nightmares," I said, but feeling treacherous: her observation sounded so exact—for Brand.

But *she* wasn't listening now.

"He didn't *want* to get rid of those nightmares. He wanted to suffer them, they were real to him, they were like *things* he could touch and believe in though none of us could see them. But he did. And how could he deny what he knew he was see-ing. They were there."

She virtually stopped then, turning my curiosity, then satis-faction, to discomfort now that she'd reached what was to her too a kind of climax.

"The nightmares took him from me. In a perverse way he preferred them."

The restaurant was empty. One waiter a hanger-on to clear the last tables waited if not impatiently, bored but courteous.

"Nobody prefers them," I reiterated, "though nightmares are a terrible kind of magic. You're fascinated by what's in you no matter how perverse and have to follow where it leads. Brand must have."

"Perhaps. You knew him best, you knew his mind and

thoughts, but Esther and I . . . I don't understand him any more now than before. I wish I did. I hope you do. Do you?"

"I— We're too close to it yet. And you know me—I fear hasty judgments."

"But you feel."

"Yes, and fear. I'm emotional too. If I move too fast I could blunder and be terribly unfair to Brand, and he's the last person in the world I want to be unjust with, the very last. It would be—"

Unfair to myself.

I dared not say that. It would lead into an internal labyrinth with, for Sylvia, a dead end. Or perhaps it was too early to pursue it. I had the others to see and a long way to go. And I had to restrain myself. I was too eager to follow Brand and in my zeal feared I'd miss some detail, clue, key that would somehow restore him.

So, the last, we closed the place. On the way home she was silent. She had gone this route too many times with Brand, so he was too much with us. And after my refusing a nightcap at her place (I felt her own weary reluctance, for she had failed with both of us as I had with both of them, and she must have felt that), she drove me to Esther's. The city was quiet, the sky darker for the stars that teased, sparkling, the air so clean after the rain, and streets, buildings, lights, everything beautiful and too pristine.

Something—I think we both were aware—had ended. There would be—there was now—no reason why we should meet again. We had exhausted a relationship. Brand had brought us to what we might have admitted long before, but for his relationship with Sylvia. And I would seldom be back. With Brand gone, except for my parents, there would be little reason. I realized then how nearly completely my life now belonged in Madrid. Never had Carmen so transcended the moment. It was as if I had been waiting unconsciously for this liberation too bittersweet and impossible to realize fully without her. I longed for her. I had to talk to her.

"I've been waiting," she said. "I knew something vital was happening to you. After all, Brand was such a part of your life."

"Brand was what bound us all. I used to think it was me the traveler who kept us all in touch."

"You were. But he was the magnet. They were all drawn to him—and I was too. You couldn't get out of that orbit—why would you want to?—as long as Brand was the center."

"Sun."

"Exactly. . . . You haven't been to Bristol yet?"

"I'm postponing it—till last. Esther's frantic about Rich, more upset than she lets on. He's with his grandmother, so I'm going to Huntsville. He's wound up so tight, Esther says, he may crack, so the sooner the better. If I can get him to let go, simply let out what's bottled up in him and relieve the pressure—"

"I'd say you were a good samaritan if the talk wasn't to relieve you too."

I laughed at her always uncompromising directness. I count on her never making the truth fuzzy.

"You, thank heaven, don't let me feel self-pity."

"It's why you're with me."

"One reason."

"Now who doesn't compromise?"

"And that's why I'm with you."

"Love's what it is."

Again, in that deep clarity of voice, from the diaphragm, which I so admire in Spanish women, she said, "Love has no definition. It's what we don't question. If it weren't love, you wouldn't have answered Brand's grandfather's call. Let's leave it at that."

"I don't know how long this will take me."

"No matter. I'll be waiting. And why? It's what I don't know. It just *is*." She laughed, deep.

"I count on it."

"You have it."

"I love it."

"Me too." I heard her kiss. "You!" And returned it. "I'll call."

The morning after Sylvia, I flew to Huntsville. The trip was as much to see Mrs. Brand as to see Rich. In my vision Brand's father stood always behind him like the overlapping in a double exposure, like a second person whose outline follows the edge of his own so you're not quite sure whether there is one figure or two there. And Mrs. Brand was always like a shadow cast on the lawn beside them, the inevitable silent presence, invisible but for that shadow. I say silent because she would never betray him whether from love or respect or fear or even history, from an emotional bond too intricate for a peripheral person to dare to try to unravel.

Over the phone the day before, however, she had been effusive, warm, and charming, motherly, with eagerness in her voice —perhaps on Rich's account though she too, like the others, made me feel she had been expecting me.

"It lacks only your coming," she said, meaning, I supposed, that with me the missing element here at last, Brand's death and burial would be complete. Finished. But never forgotten.

Mrs. Brand and Rich were at the airport. I expected them. What I didn't expect, since I hadn't seen Rich in a good long time, was the very tall and dark man standing beside her, dressed almost too formally for the occasion—suit, tie, topcoat (for Mrs. Brand surely?).

The sight halted me just long enough to catch myself thinking *Mr. Brand*.

The hair and skin so dark were Mr. Brand's.

Yet the height was Brand's.

In seconds the boy was moving toward me, smiling, while she waited beyond.

"Ferris!"

"Rich!"

With her waiting as always in the background, pendant, effaced, this might have been Brand's and my arrival years ago, after our high school graduation.

When I approached, she took my shoulders and pressed her face to mine.

"You're so good to come. Nothing could please us more—not, Rich?"

Us.

Something was beginning, or had begun, I thought. Or perhaps she was merely being very much the grandmother, or too much the mother, vigilant because of Rich's trauma since having discovered Brand dead in his studio.

On the way to the house—Rich was driving, he made no talk—she said, "Tell me about Madrid and your travels and your work and Carmen."

At the house Rich was quiet the evening long while she talked on with that charm she could so cleverly use to veneer those little reverberations and twitches of nerves if she ceased talking for too long. Her nervous eyes, a lovely gray blue, were secure only when they were fixed unflaggingly on me, when her modulations were most comfortable—social or sincere—as if she were drawing confidence from my interest, which itself was a confidence in her conversation. As she talked, I felt Rich withdraw as pronouncedly as a razor crab edging into sand and felt too in her kind insistence on what I couldn't really call entertaining me the curious presence of her husband as if she were aware of his watching her. Perhaps Rich's presence partially restored her husband to her. Since she had been for so many years denied both the boys' visits and had not lived their personal history (which could not *live* for her), she must have known no other recourse than to conduct herself with them as she had conducted herself with her husband and Brand. She had control. Yet she seemed then, and would for the next two days, verbally pitched, her voice on the edge of breaking, and visually perched, sitting precariously on the edge of the sofa or chairs—I felt if she leaned too far forward or ventured too deeply into her own emotions, she might break, spill. Eventually she did. I knew she would. With her husband gone, and Brand, she had no reason for fear now. She could hurt neither. Neither could hurt her. Neither could hurt the other.

That night, however, it was Rich I was more concerned

about—for himself first, for Esther, and ultimately for me, what I could gather of Brand. I had thought when Rich met me at the airport he'd embrace me in a release of emotion, but he'd held that off with a handshake. At home, after we'd exhausted talk of his mother, her art, with some "notes" on Ralph (whom he did like and whose productive relationship with his mother he approved of, even admired and maybe in his own isolation envied), and my own plans, Mrs. Brand, certain I was tired by then, said, "Come, Ferris." Rich had carried my bag off on arrival. "I've put you in Paul's old room since Rich prefers the guest room." I glanced at Rich. Quick, his glance crossed mine, faltering but fleeting. If only she hadn't been with us, *he might release it*, I thought. But he said, "Goodnight, Ferris" and I "Goodnight, Rich" and followed Mrs. Brand to that room I had occupied with Brand after graduation thirty years before.

I was afraid direct questions would unnerve Rich, though I had some doubts about any other approach since he'd set up a defense, dense. I had to count on my persistent presence building up an emotional atmosphere that would cause him to give way. I was anxious because behind it all I felt the call of Brand himself. Confidence would be difficult with the three of us moving around in that uncomfortable comfort of old courtesies.

And then on the second afternoon light broke in. I said, "It's been years since I've been to the Museum of Modern Art. They've got a number of your mother's pieces I'd like to see again. How about it, Rich?"

I held my breath: Mrs. Brand begged off.

The paintings were in a new wing, recently opened to the public. Standing before one of her familiar early pieces, I said, "Your father met your mother here. Did you know that? This painting was in that show."

He stared at the painting. He was agitated. I thought his eyes filled, but he angled his head away from me.

I said, "He was just about your age then, Rich, and just beginning. He was on his first job, but his preparation was equivalent to years of experience. He knew photography—

everything. It was his obsession from the first—he ate, drank, dreamed photography. He was already one of the best—he'd made himself. It only remained for the world to recognize it, and it very quickly did."

Abruptly he turned and left the salon, crossed the corridor, and went outside. I watched him cross the patch of lawn and sit on one of the stone benches.

In a few minutes I followed. I came up behind. Bent forward, elbows on his knees, he was clutching his hands. I pressed a hand on his shoulder. He dropped his head.

"Why'd he do that to me, Ferris?"

The question startled.

Brand, you have no right to do this to me.

"Do what?"

"Leave me with *that*. Let me find him that way. Did he think I'd never forget? I won't, I can't—I never will."

"He couldn't have intended you to find him that way."

"Why do you say that? How do you know he didn't plan it that way?"

No, not Brand.

"Your father wasn't cruel."

"He was expecting me. He *said* at the studio. You don't do it that way unless you plan it. It was too conspicuous. He may have done it—I think that sometimes—to make that horror unforgettable. . . . It was! I can't get it out of my mind. He was sitting so straight in his chair. His head was as shiny as glass. It was almost inhuman. I didn't know what it was. I wasn't sure it was my father—his shape, yes—until I went close and touched his head. I had to."

"That doesn't mean he planned it—or for *you*. You can't know what he was thinking when he talked to you or what happened between the time he talked to you and his decision to do it, what smallest detail . . ."

"But he left me *that*—"

Image, I thought.

"And you have to accept that, and bear it. We must. Whatever his intention, he left it to us too, through you. But if you *are* right and he did it for you, you have to make of it what you can. Surely, Rich, he did it to make you strong, not weak."

"I keep trying to figure it out, but reliving it is maddening."

"Think what it must have been for him."

"I try to imagine how it was for him. It's too hard. I can't."

"Don't try. Let it come in its own good time. I'd like to know how it was too. I need to."

He was grateful, I could tell, to keep talking and get that moment out. He said his heart made a bolt of "mortal terror" when he saw the figure far behind the glass didn't move, and still didn't when he broke the pane and reached in and opened the door. "Dad? It's me. What's happened? What's wrong? Dad? Dad!" He said afterwards he realized he'd been talking to his father all the time. "When I touched his head, I stopped. It was so quiet I heard *me* thunder like I'd touched *my* head. It took me a time standing there before I had sense enough to know what to do—"

"Your mother told me . . . the rest, and the funeral." In Bristol. Brand had desired to be in the place he'd genuinely loved, where his true spiritual parents were—as if, I thought, in death he could escape the terrain of his passion (love as hate can) for his father and his love, crippled too, for his mother.

Now with Rich's silence the noise of the traffic coming and going in the public parking lot across the street and the steps and voices of visitors to the museum returned the day to us. *Nothing*, the clear grass and walks, the unmarred waters of the spring, the indifferent breeze, the courthouse high on the square seemed to say, *nothing has happened*.

Rich said, "After they took him away, I sat in his chair. I tried to imagine—" He began to cry, great heaves and chokes.

I left him to himself and walked around the lagoon.

When I came back, he was smiling. He was at least momentarily liberated, for the first time physically at ease with me, not melancholy, as if he'd actually coughed up a phlegm that had stymied breath. He looked actually taller. That impression of inside huddling was gone. At least, I thought, one skin had been peeled away.

He said, "You're the only father I have now. He must have counted on that too."

"Or counted on your being a son."

"Son?"

"To your grandmother."

"Yes. But she counted on you, Ferris—to make her believe. I don't mean she can't believe he's gone, or can't believe that my grandfather's gone, twice. I mean if I'm here, and you, she can't believe in *ends*. They died, but *didn't*, because we're here."

"But I'm not—"

"She *said* you. *Ferris* she said. And you weren't here then. But you were *somewhere*, she said, and you make them come alive to her, you're the proof. It's her memory of war, the nightmare. She's afraid of extermination. She's *been* afraid of destruction without any trace. She fears losing the *last* sign of anything that verifies that he was actually here. Even the grave doesn't convince her. She's afraid—was always afraid—one day the world will turn on my grandfather and the Germans here for what they did to *us*."

Us.

Esther. Esther's. Jews.

"You understand all that?" I said.

"You forget who I am."

"Who you are?"

"There's more of him in me than you know."

Brand's son Brand.

Had Brand feared that what was in his father was in his son?

"That's why you spend so much time with your grandmother?"

"Part. The loss was too sudden. And she'll never be sure why my father did it. Or what it means. And because she can't, she imagines too many possibilities. With her sensibility you can imagine her feelings. She's been over the edge and back so many times in her life that she can't rest. Seeing me gives her some. And don't think my visits are all for her, oh no, they're for me too. I need her, and *him*. Dean. As long as my father was alive, Dean—something of Dean—was. I'd never really let him go. I didn't brood. My father kept me from it. But when I saw my father sitting so stark still in that chair—I didn't think it then, I was almost incapable of thought when I found him, but my blood knew—Dean *really* died at that instant. Maybe that's what left me numb. If at first Dad's death brought them both too close, it got to be unbearable because when my father cut himself off, that cut me off *physically* from both him and Dean for good. It made it undeniable *fact*. That was the blow. I've been out of it—till now. My mother said you'd come. She said it would make a difference. Don't do anything foolish, she said, wait. You see, *she* knows I'm too much his son, not hers."

"She's wiser than she can say."

"She senses."

"Call it that. Anyway she was right."

"She knew you'd come. I was waiting. It's been worth it." He gazed off over the lagoon to the courthouse. "And is it for you?"

The maturity of his question surprised me. I don't know why I hadn't expected it—he'd so obviously thought out as far as he could his father's death. He granted me a more analytical curiosity than I actually have.

"You mean—am I wiser now?"

"Exactly."

"You think I came for that?"

"No. I know you came for me. Being Dad's lifelong friend, you'd have reason to come even if it weren't for me. But I gave you double reason."

"Yes."

"So, are you?"

"Wiser now?"

"Yes."

Now in my thoughts was the son, what was *in* the son that Brand might have feared was there—surely what he'd feared in himself. Now I suspected that Rich might have sensed my thoughts. "Shall we leave it at that?"

"Enough said—for now." He smiled and gripped my hand. I hoped that meant *I can begin now*. Because he could.

He could leave now—had to go back to the university to teach—for Ohio. His break was over. Sunday night he had to leave his grandmother "—to you, Ferris, I'm glad to say. I was afraid she'd be alone too suddenly—and she will—but as short as your visit will be—" I'd said till Tuesday. "—you'll help her through. She depends—"

"And you don't?"

"Me too. But I don't have her history."

"Oh yes you do. You're part of it. You weren't there but, more than you think, it's made you."

"*That*—" *That* was the moment in the studio in Providence. "—made me realize how events do help make you, so I think more about them now—the Hitler war, Jews, my grandfather, our name, and Dean, and *him*. But no more of that. Not now. Okay?"

On the way to the airport—he was driving—he might have been seeing that scene in the space ahead. *Don't*, I'd have said, but refrained. It would appear and appear, less frequently of course, all his life. It would leave its mark on his character.

Alone with me, in the next two days Mrs. Brand turned mother, but unimposing, a friend close if casual. I understood Rich's comfort with her, why Brand must never have felt distraught when with her, a refuge from his father's unflagging firmness. Set against his father's fixed attitudes, his mother's must have seemed flimsy and unsubstantial, and Brand must always have found it difficult to offer anything concrete in defense against his father's demands.

I would be two days listening to his mother off and on. I don't mean to give the impression that she talked without interruption. I tell it in the order it comes to me, though it came from her in bits and meanders and sometimes in bursts, almost harangues, or little floods of emotion, or sporadic afterthoughts whenever an object or word triggered her memory. At times she groped almost in the kind of madness which she now—and sometimes Brand talking about her over the years—confessed to.

"What could we expect?"

She set her coffee down on the glass tabletop. We were having breakfast on the sun porch.

"Heinrich was always militant, very, and handsome when he was being most strict. Peculiarly, it became him." She smiled nostalgically. "But it never became me, and never Paul. Paul was too much me. His sensibilities were mine, and his looks mine, my family's. And Rich's sensibilities too, but not his looks —he could have been Heinrich's true son. One look at him is enough to tell that. And my husband suffered from that; he couldn't believe such a reproduction of himself could be . . . could have other blood. With his training and his loyalty he couldn't help—oh he couldn't, Ferris—believing in *blood*. He had an absolute fear of tainted blood, and of anything that wasn't clearly envisioned or executed. Purity was a religion with him, and *before* Hitler. Hitler paved a way for his own religion— narrow, I can say now that he's dead. But I loved him. I was blinded by my love—still am. I adored and with the same futile —I can say that now too—and destructive devotion. And look what his faith brought him to. It brought Paul the same single-mindedness that *he'*d had, and in that sense—isn't it strange?— we couldn't have been more alive, none of us, because we were so obsessed. It was our bond. Heinrich needed adoration, I needed to adore. How we both depended on that! Ay, Ferris, how weak we were! Weak. How often the weak seem strong. That was our tragedy . . . and Paul's. His father never forgave him that blood, never. If a man could hate his own so—"

"No." I had to interrupt, not for Brand's sake but for hers. How could I console?

"Don't, Ferris. Listen— His wasn't hate from love. He had cut Paul off. If he could have, he'd have *done something* to Paul and Esther and the boys to show his hate for that blood. You don't know hate, Ferris. Few people know such hate. You must understand—in a way it was the worst hatred of all, hellish, pure hell, but you must understand *not for him* because he hated from pride. He wasn't, as anyone would say, too proud to admit he was wrong, because his pride was absolute even after we lost the war and came here to what he never stopped considering enemy territory, living with other Germans whom he called, but only in his little circle here at home, the repentant ones. Oh, his pride was absolute. That meant he was absolutely right, so how with his faith in his pride, which Hitler had personified, could he have been wrong. Never! Oh, never! How many years—to the very last breath—he believed! He clung to a few because they shared his unflagging faith in what we had lost and in a social upheaval that would revive that vanished world. He believed with the same conviction others await the second coming of a messiah. What maddened me—I think Heinrich knew—was that I couldn't know what he'd actually done before being sent to Peenemünde. But there were . . . we . . . he wouldn't speak. That was proof enough, or fear enough, for us. How far could you go? You could kill without lifting a finger. He would *defend* the atrocities, but he would turn furious if we asked a direct question, rage. You don't need to touch to murder—just *nod* or *sign* or *say*, a flick of a lid, that's enough. And I—I never could be sure—could doubt, but *not*. If I did, I would be destroying with what I didn't *know* was true, and I knew what his steel will was capable of when it touched his pride in pride itself.

"I can't say I was numbed by his views, as antagonistic as I felt to them, as Paul was. Despite Paul's near reverence for his father as authority, I'd had enough inklings of that hatred over the years in his casual inferences and occasional lengthy confidences, though he never approached details so intimate that they'd undermine his father forever in my feelings—or in his own because he wanted to believe only in his father's positive side. Unwilling as Paul himself was to hate, *hating* hate itself, he willed against hating his father—he hated his ideas. Why . . . you will wonder, Ferris, why I dare tell this—how I can—

why now." *Why?* but to justify Paul, who had escaped him and who might in some way have betrayed him. "Besides," she said, "he had too much honest respect for himself and me to blur or tarnish or corrode our deep friendship by imposing a weight he'd carried and which he felt he alone should carry, though I'd have borne it willingly enough at any time and he knew that."

It now occurred to me that Brand later feared the weight of his father's past on his sons, because if he'd felt it with such devastation, wouldn't they? And wouldn't *their* devastation be his *ultimate* devastation? Still, it was typical of him—out of sheer courtesy, part of his innate gentleness or gentility, a true gentleman in his father's old traditional sense—that he was too considerate to pour his passion out fully and burden me. Perhaps he was aware that some burdens, once imposed, can never be withdrawn to give relief to the other.

"It's incredible how Brand could hold so much in, and conceal his feelings—"

"Because he was good. Paul wouldn't hurt *him*. And Heinrich had bet on that when he finally did let Paul go."

Then *that*, I was thinking, perhaps that—they hadn't let Brand go to Bristol to live with his grandparents earlier because they were afraid he would talk about his father, what went on; but they had almost no choice when he was older and insisted: his eruption into illness at home would have been even a greater condemnation.

"Heinrich had done Paul so much harm. Nobody could have known unless he'd lived with Paul. Paul himself didn't. Feelings come so gradually. And Heinrich was clever. Oh, he loved Paul. You can't know what confidence he had in him. Paul was going to be a model, he *was*, but he didn't turn out as Heinrich had planned. Heinrich did plan. He was all plan. As a boy Paul and his father were ideal together—in the community and with all of us who came over with Werner and later, and at home with the few close friends with whom Heinrich could . . . let his hair down? At home, always the talk was *German, Deutschland, Der*

Führer, still *tomorrow the world*. Paul grew up in that talk, at first too young to think anything of it. Heinrich never counted on Paul's growing up *out there* and being cultivated by the American world of school and slowly coming to hate the words *German* and *Nazi* and *Führer* and even the language and beginning to withdraw—camping alone then, and hiking alone, talking less at the table, above all locked away studying, his greatest excuse to escape his father. That was the irony: Heinrich preached education as the way to control and direct the society he envisioned as coming one day. It turned Paul sick. His stomach constantly bothered him, and his head—such headaches he had, unbearable—and he was nervous, though I could see how the poor boy fought to hide it—he feared punishment, he knew too well his father's indisputable authority. Paul grew too thin, and his face, how it broke out!"

I saw Brand on his first day at Bristol High, his thin torso high over the desk, rigid, that head rigid too, and his face so pimpled.

"I remember."

"Yes. You would—because by the time he went to Bristol—"

"But how?"

"How?"

"How did he convince his father to let him go?"

"Paul had reached such a critical point that *I* . . . you must understand, Ferris . . . I was sick, I *had* been ever since Peenemünde. There I'd become pregnant, and during the worst time. The Americans were bombing us, things had come to a standstill, we were all trying to get out, authority had fallen apart, and Hitler—you know the history—we had lost everything, bombed out, there was nowhere to go. And I . . . I've always had bad nerves. I was too sensitive. By then I was half-crazy—I mean seriously distracted by the bombing, my pregnancy, and Heinrich a prisoner, and I was insane to know *what* would happen. I had to go home to my parents, alone, and wait. The least thing weighing on me sends me over the edge—it's so hard to come back, such a struggle; but *he*— This is what you must understand. Naturally you'll ask, How could you stand a man with your husband's ideas? Ferris, he was always there. It was *because he was always there*—you don't know what that can mean to a woman, and especially in our circumstances— and he was never once mean to me, inexplicably good to me— inexplicably if you consider everything else—because he needed me. That was the one insane thing, reasonable but insane, that such a man could *need*, and need so desperately and completely one other and *only* the one other person by some innate law destined to be *his*. He believed that. You don't know how that weakness moved me. If we three were bound by our obsessive- ness, then *that* was *our* bond, Heinrich's and mine. He culti- vated my weakness so I'd never leave him, and I *would* not, never for a moment wanted to despite even the suspicion of horrors he so approved of and might even have perpetrated. My defense against that was always my cowardice. I sought refuge in my cowardice in the name of his need for me and mine for him, *worse* when we become war aliens, respected, desired *prisoners* of a kind, willing ones most of us, but not Heinrich and his circle; they clung to their creed.

"And when Paul was born—ah, no man ever, none, Ferris, put such hope in a son—he saw the future in Paul. You should have seen him. Paul was his life all over again. But the war and Paul's birth left me broken, nervous, half-crazy fearing and adapting to this new country. You can imagine how we Ger- mans had to cling to one another. You know your people, the prejudice, especially here in the South in this state where the lower classes and ignorance abound, though Werner and the others won them over, the quality of their work did, Werner did by being number one in the world because he dreamed of penetrating space and putting man on the moon, and did. Hein- rich would have given anything to be number one. He wasn't, so wanted Paul to be. Heinrich never told me anything about his work, never confused his work before Peenemünde or here with his homelife or social world. He was that compartmentalized. Anyone seeing him at home alone with us wouldn't have believed he was the same man. Of course he *was*—his whole life was based on his pride—pride in *purity, auf das Beste.*"

The best.

I could hear Paul, I can hear him now, telling me that: "Day after day in school my father drove it into me. 'Nothing is worth it, Paul, unless you're the best, not among *them*—' With a fling of his arm his father dismissed the northwest section of blacks and poor whites, shacks, cheap housing, cultural trash. '—but anywhere, everywhere, among Nordics and Aryans.' He loved to say those words."

But not Paul. When he spoke them, his voice fell, humiliated, as always when he uttered his father's words *Nordics, Aryans.*

"Heinrich never tired," she said. "He drove Paul, poor Paul, till he too was all nerves, though like his father Paul had remarkable control. He never fell apart like me at each crisis and more and more at smaller ones. That control saved him because he too was firm in his determinations. How many times *you* must have seen that, Ferris! And when he could bear his father's harping no more, he stood up against him: he *would* live in Bristol with his grandmother and grandfather, he would *not* go to school, he would run away; but the worst threat was that he *would not study.* He had his father there. Heinrich was almost insane: Paul, 'my own son,' had thrown his own weapon, education, at him. Paul bribed him. 'If you don't let me go, I'll flunk out.' Paul was no fool—he knew his father's pride in his name and in *him,* and his fear of denigration by his neighbors and the public and of course the rocket team as well as the whole world of 'the Von Braun Hilton' at Redstone. But his father would *not* be destroyed—and by his own son—after he had taught him this very independence for his, Heinrich's, own pride in him! What Heinrich couldn't understand was that Paul hated what Heinrich loved *him* for, that pride in him. Paul wanted Heinrich's love, but he refused even then to be a product of hate. Oh, Paul had insight. In fact, he feared his own insight so he seldom spoke it; it kept him knotted up inside, like me. But he came to understand his father's pride. Though

Heinrich never called his own pride hate, Paul knew his father loved that hate and coddled it like a child, and Paul would *not* be that child. When Paul went, Heinrich was sure Paul hated him. Heinrich had already had proof of Paul's superiority—his perfect grades. He hadn't counted on Paul's determination to offset our foreignness and become *pure* American, never to speak German outside the house. He had to at home always. Heinrich wouldn't put up with English except when anybody came in, so Paul consciously clung to English, loved English, shunned any trace of accent. Do you know, Ferris, once he'd gone to Bristol I'd never heard him speak a word of German until after Heinrich's death."

"I can believe that. I never heard him speak German, though he must have when alone with his grandparents."

As *she* talked more and more, somewhat excitedly, her own German broke through.

"And when Esther changed the boys' name, Heinrich lost control—I shudder to remember his fury—and shouted at her, insulted her. He was never more the child than then. He broke down after and wept in my arms, *mein kind* I couldn't explain, all my life with him trying to, and wanting to break the shell— what his parents may have done to him, what he was born to, so aristocratic and aloof and superior. How *was* he, Ferris? Day and night it haunts me. I could never admit to myself that my love wouldn't release him from a staunchness as taut as twisted wire. I thought love begot love. Fool idea! But I was as stubborn as he. I'd never admit to myself what he felt for me was not love as I imagined it, but my own need to depend. *I* was responsible for that. I *wanted* him to seize and never let go, believing that eventually need would breed that love, love yes, but not *how*. He fed love to feed himself. What was so terrible, maybe the worst thing, was—he wouldn't learn. There are such people, Ferris. He was one, the more pitiful for that. And I was too nervous and sick. He helped make me so. Paul knew that. *He* loved me. He was afraid for me. But Paul was smart—he could have been my victim, the victim of my weakness, and clung to save me for my own self; but Paul was too strong for that yet *not* too strong to save himself from his father, because his father pursued him, yes he did. By leaving him, didn't Paul realize he was binding himself to his father by guilt? That guilt he could never escape. He always suffered from the break. And marrying a Jew made it irreparable. The marriage strengthened his conscience, the one thing he claimed his father did *not* have, would never have, though he never knew how that marriage destroyed his father. Conscience was the great difference between them, Paul claimed, his gift from me. His *softness*, he called it; his father called it *weakness*. But the gift was not a gift, but a lie. Did I have a conscience? Did I? If I have now, it is only because it *came*, it came with Paul's . . . death. *He* gave it to me, he . . .

"But I wonder—it drives me half crazy sometimes—if it was that conscience that killed Paul. But how? Was it that trial? What could that have to do with him? Was it that, Ferris? Was it?"

I'd have given anything to say *yes* and satisfy her, and satisfy myself too, end it. But I couldn't lie to her. It would be lying to myself. It would be no answer, useless, and achieve nothing. And she would know that.

"I can't answer that. Part, surely. He couldn't tear himself away from the trial."

"But why? The world is full of murderers."

"He didn't believe the boy was a murderer, or only half-believed it. Ferris believed the boy was as innocent as he was guilty, or simply didn't know, and that dilemma possessed him as if it were his."

"His?"

"Yes. You knew his capacity for feeling so deeply that he identified with people."

How she stared past me, out the window! I could see the window in her eyes. The sill cut across them like the horizon of a still sea.

"Yes."

"*Why* his?

"Because he could never know the boy's guilt or innocence."

"Why should that matter so to him? Nobody can be absolutely sure of another's . . ."

She faltered.

"Exactly."

I couldn't be sure either.

How many times, Brand, had you considered suicide? How close had you come? At what precise moment had you decided to do it at last?

I wondered how many times when I was with him I might have shunted myself away from some sign of that thought in him, and so turned toward that decision.

She said, "Paul wouldn't speak of that boy's trial, not to me. He day after day brooded alone. I never knew anything to possess him so. And he piled up photos. He'd stare at them by the hour, waiting, as if they could tell him something. He was so bewildered. Did he talk to you about it?"

"Yes."

"And what?"

"What I said: the boy seemed as innocent as he was guilty. Brand couldn't decide. He thought his actions sprang from the same source. And to him the jury was doing what that boy did, killing, and without really knowing the truth, so he felt the jury was guilty and innocent too. Brand couldn't bear that."

"Can't you guess why?"

"No."

"Then he *didn't* tell you. He didn't go far enough with you."

"He told me about his work—what he wanted."

"Not his work, no. About *him*. He never said? No. Paul understood, oh too well, adoration. You don't understand adoration, Ferris. No. Adoration rejects you, the self—*I* know—because only the other exists. It was cultivated death. And death is worse than madness."

"Paul didn't think so."

"Because he had *courage*. Most people wouldn't do what he did."

"Because they believe in sin."

"And Paul believed in *us*, or wanted to."

"You lose me."

"I'll tell you, then. Paul was convinced *he* was responsible."

"For that boy?"

"That boy? *Not*. For much more—many—since, yes, he was tortured, convinced his father at some time had killed, though he never knew—there was no way he could have found out— what his father did during the war, *before* Peenemünde. I don't know *what* Paul knew. Who could tell him? *Who* would know but his father? Not even *I*, Ferris. Not even I . . . Do you know what that must have meant to Paul?"

I quivered at the thought of what horrors Brand must have imagined, or even known.

"Or to me?" Her voice sank to a low murmur. "It meant— *you* know how deeply Paul felt things—he was part, but part of what? If his father *had* killed, *he* had. He was as responsible as his father—*for* his father. And for *me*. After all, he and I were his father's. How could he separate us from him? He had to live with that every day. And I did. You can't kill thoughts! After the trial—you can't know what it was like to be me whenever he looked at me—it was as if his father had come to life and he made me realize *again*, years after he'd died, how I too was responsible for what his father did. More and more I could see the pity for me. He kept his distance. I saw he didn't want to. It hurt him. I saw his pain. He would look far off, but oh I caught those evasions—he'd turn his head in pain but I could do nothing, say nothing."

I said, "But he was closer to you than anybody. Brand never talked love, but showed it. When he mentioned you, he couldn't hide his affection."

"Or hate—if for his father, then for me too, because his father and I shared, we were the same thing—and hate's the same as love—hate hurts too, it never lets up, it's too deep. The same. It is, isn't it? Or why always the same suffering, the same—"

"Paul wouldn't have suffered if he hadn't cared."

"Too much!—all his life, poor boy, and worse at the end

133

because he had failed his father as his father had failed him. He was not *der Beste*—that's what he realized. Paul said so. All the days his father preached *be the best*, nothing else counts, that's what it meant, not only *Blutbrüderschaft*, but the brotherhood of the best only, all the best. Paul shouted that out after the trial when he collapsed. You'd just gone back to Madrid. I thought he was on his way to regaining not just his strength but a whole new attitude now that the terrible nightmare—he took the trial as a personal nightmare—was over and he could set his mind on other things. He shouted, 'He was *never* the best, my father, he wanted to be, he was associated with the best in his field, but *he* wanted to be Wernher von Braun—that's what the best is— to be *one*, only *one*—and he wasn't that but a satellite, one of many. The best rocket team—yes, team. He gained from that . . . illusions. But he knew. It's what killed my father. I *know* it did. It had to—or he'd have killed himself one day because he couldn't stand to fail, and he *had*, as his Germany had failed, and failed a second time because his dream for it was already doomed.' Paul said that, something like that, Ferris. But *why* did he? What did Paul want, Ferris? What did to be the best mean to him? He had an international reputation. What photographer could do more?"

I didn't answer. However, I was not really there for her. Once started, she was questioning herself. She couldn't stop talking to herself.

"Well, he didn't want it, then. He wanted something else. And he couldn't have it, could he?"

I couldn't say: There are no limits, the struggle's our disease and our joy.

Perhaps we're no more than flies battering against the pane, finally. But if you're a fly, you go at it till the struggle kills you.

"*Could* he?" Her voice rose as she rose and went to the window. She might have been appealing to something out there, calling out of her own confusion.

I was afraid for her. *She crosses over*, Brand had said. Yet talk might keep her from that.

"No, he couldn't." She turned—she was talking to me now. "And do you know how I know? Of course you don't—you'd gone. It was after that trial and his collapse. He was getting better. I thought he was. And his body *was*, but I hadn't realized how agitated his mind was until the day before he went back to Bristol. He had to go, he said, it was his place, he had so much work to do. 'In Bristol! What work?' I asked him. After all, his studio was in Providence, though he'd virtually abandoned it since he was always on the go, all over the world. 'You don't work in Bristol,' I said. I shouldn't have, because that's what triggered him—"

She halted, with that sudden forlorn look, absent, that made me fear she would bog down, lose track, and not go on.

"What do you mean *triggered*?"

"His fury—"

"Brand's? But he was never violent."

"Oh, he was that day. Turned on me, shouted—at *me*. 'I do work. I do nothing *but* work in Bristol.' That's how I knew his mind was still on that case, distracted. I supposed he'd never come back, if the truth was known. Oh, he was sorry after, apologized, almost in tears. That made me realize how—still!—he had other things on his mind, because *always* he had more control. That control was his father in him, but in letting go, that sign of weakness, I recognized *me*. But 'nothing *but* work in Bristol'! 'What work?' I said. *I* was upset by his shouting because it was unheard of from him, and confused and a little frightened, though I shouldn't have been. After all, he'd been sick. Still, he'd been cranky, critical, picking at me, and complained not only during the trial but before, each time he'd wasted coming home during the year, maybe because of everything else happening in the world, as if he'd been storing up his fury and could let it go at last. 'What's there to photograph in Bristol?' I said. 'Photograph?' He looked at me as if I were crazy. *He* looked crazy then. 'Photograph!' he cried. 'Did I say photograph? Did I? *No*, I did not. And to show you—' We were in the kitchen. He dashed to his room and came back with his

135

camera, went out the kitchen door to the garage. I stood there looking after him. He came back with the camera and smashed and smashed and smashed till it was unrecognizable. *He* was. He wasn't *with* me. He'd smashed it as if he were beating him with it—"

She caught my movement, and stared at me.

"Yes, you too—you guess it, don't you?

I couldn't say no.

Him, she'd said.

I nodded.

"I was so *sure*. He was striking out at Heinrich. It was some kind of retribution. He wanted to destroy him—he *was* destroying him. *I* knew it. Paul was aware that I knew. He was trying to rid himself of his father once and for all. He stood gazing down at the camera. He had many cameras, but that one he never let out of his sight. He stood there a long time. His stillness scared me. I went to my room, but all I could think was—it had never occurred to me before—that he'd never taken a portrait of his father, not one existed. And he couldn't now he was dead."

She was crying softly.

Was Paul furious because he'd never taken a photo of his father? Then it was too late, he couldn't photograph his father, and if he'd had no photos, he couldn't tear up his father, he couldn't efface him, he'd never die—?

"Forgive me, Ferris, I didn't mean to—"

"I've been feeling like doing that myself."

She smiled. "You're consoling me. What a blessing you were to Paul."

"And wasn't he to me?"

"Of course. What else?"

"You don't have to tell me what hurts you."

"But I did, *do*—and to you."

"Why me?"

"You. Don't you know why? Because there's nobody in the world I can tell but you."

"Not Rich?"

136

"No, not yet. He's too young. He's not ready. He's too sensitive, like Paul, and he's just had the worst blow. In the wake of that— No, it will take time. One day . . . There are things the young aren't ready to handle. At this moment Rich isn't. Besides, you're as near as I can get to Paul. Oh, Ferris, his life—and Heinrich's too—would have been so much easier if Paul had had a brother from the beginning."

I turned away toward the valley below and the far mountains. The ridge of deep trees blurred gray in the gray sky.

"He left the camera lying on the garage floor. I didn't touch it. I was afraid to. To him it must have been a live thing he'd killed. But in the morning it was gone—in the trash, I suppose. I didn't ask. I wouldn't upset him more. It was his last morning . . . here . . ."

She couldn't go on.

After a while I said, "I was traveling then. I got the news very late. I'm sure you'd learned that."

"Oh, yes. My father told me. They both lamented it because they were sure how hurt you'd be. It was as much to have you here as a matter of conscience and loyalty to Paul. How they loved him! Sometimes I think he was their son, and my husband was not. How twisted life can be."

"So tangled we can't unravel it sometimes, but we have to work at that. It's all we have, everything."

"Or nothing."

The house, full as it was—gracious and beautiful—must have seemed a wasteland to her and now, with my going, bleak; if my presence brought Paul and Mr. Brand close yet staved them off, at my leaving they would crowd back in. Memory consoles, and harries.

Yet she smiled rather stoically when afternoon came, took my hand, held it.

"You're sure you won't let me take you to the airport?"

I insisted no.

Just before the taxi came, she said, "Ah, I'm forgetting the packet," and went to find it.

"I took this from Paul when he was sick. He believed Rich had taken it to Providence. I forgot to give them to Paul so he went back to Providence without them. He called. I said I'd mail them, but by the time I got around to it . . . They're yours. My father said Paul left his personal things to you."

When the taxi arrived, she kissed me, on the edge of breaking. She looked, tall as she was, so frail standing bone thin in the doorway, in that house isolated too by its own private road and set against the valley below and the mountains beyond.

On the plane I opened the packet.

I went cold.

The execution photos.

The crowd.

Faces and faces and faces.

You should have seen the faces, Ferris.

So the photographs *had* been in the house the last time I'd been with him, during his recuperation . . .

The photos were dark, night, each with a cut of the crowd. Faces stood bold, some shadowed, some rawly lit. The eyes were glints in face after face. The faces were blobs of light breaking through rents in the darkness. But from mouths and teeth and eyes you could not distinguish rage or fear or triumph or compassion or resentment or pity or despair. I saw Brand's point—light moves and dark moves in endless conflict, indifferent. Passion. In everything. But something moves *it*. In us it breaks out *for* or *against, in the name of*, changing things, itself unchanged, indifferent. The faces were monstrous. The photos were maps of emotion.

But the light repeated in the eyes of all the faces in every photo was nothing but light. I saw what he had always before him, the two Goya paintings of the crowds of pilgrims trudging to the shrine of San Isidro to ask the maddest of impossible possibilities, a miracle. If he could have put the photos together into one mass photo and captured the whole crowd outside the jail at Galt's execution at Atmore . . . He saw light buried under darkness and in dense flesh but breaking through those eyes, through rents in the veil of flesh and clothes, rents in darkness itself . . .

The eyes—it was the light—were the same . . .

It's that I wanted to capture.

And if I failed . . . If nobody else sees it?

I wanted to. And I did. But it was not in the photo. That had been his dread, and it was mine now. I imagined that motion. I *read* it there because I knew Brand had seen it there at the moment of the boy's execution. He *had* seen. He'd described what he'd seen. He saw what was indisputably, inseparably, ugly and beautiful. He saw, I believe, what simply inexplicably *is*. And he couldn't bear it.

He had failed.

He knew even before he had seen those developed photos that he had failed.

I couldn't shape it. My eye saw it different.

He could not shape.

Brand, I thought, it's not for *that* you committed suicide? For he had struggled years to shape his vision. And he *had* had a vision of the nature of things, a glimpse—more, no matter how real or true, than most of us ever would. But more does not satisfy; it goads for still more.

He'd been certain he was getting closer—and he was close to it—*in someone else*—in Esther and Goya and the genius of painters.

For a moment in the plane soaring so smoothly I thought of *his* flight. It had taken him to that trial which he could no more resist than a moth the light. He had finally gone too close to it with his own invisible wings. Too close to what—the very heart of passion? Had his father also been driven? And had the son felt a victim not only of his own desires but of his father's like the son in the Brueghel painting, with flimsy wings constructed of feathers and wax by his father. His father had sent him, and the son had flown off course too close to the very noise of silence at the passionate center of things, and fallen. I saw Brand break, fall, flounder—end in the infinite sea. I would no longer be able to look at that painting with the old inspiration but only with lament.

It filled me with ineffable sadness.

I picked up my other suitcase at Esther's, took the bus to Bristol, and spent the next day with my mother on Hope Street before going to the Stockmanns'. I called with anxiety and dread. *I* was too close now. I wanted to be close, but feared it too. I was afraid the visit would come to nothing, yet wanted knowledge of Brand I had no right to—unless he'd chosen to yield it up by leaving a sign. But who *would* at such a desperate moment? And why?

The way through town to Brand's, crossing the Common, is only eight blocks; but I would swear the journey took years.

Ah, Carmen, how right you were!

A block from our house on Hope Street, the main artery that runs from Warren through Bristol to The Ferry and over the Mount Hope bridge to Portsmouth and Newport beyond, is the high school. Passing, I imagined Brand sitting at his desk that first day, saw us night after night at the Rogers Free Library across the street from the school, saw us Friday nights at the Pastime Theater when the high school crowd invaded the movies and during the show made so much noise Miss Osterberg the ticket lady walked the aisles turning the flashlight on the noisy ones or turning the house lights up if the gangs wouldn't quiet down.

At the Common I crossed into the world before Brand—by the courthouse, the playground, and the three grade schools I'd passed through to get to junior high at the Warren end of town. The Common was where all the great events took place, carnivals and circuses and band concerts on the green bandstand in the heart of the square (only shades of the fun, my grandparents and my mother'd say, when the old traveling minstrel shows came with whites with blacked-up nigger faces telling jokes and dancing and singing and then selling patent medicines for a dollar a bottle under signs that recalled "Lydia Pinkham's Pink Pills for Pale People"). The Common was also the place of public commemorative ceremonies, presidents' birthdays, and holy days celebrated by the Italians from Our Lady of Mount Carmel's off the Common and the Portuguese from St. Elizabeth's around the corner and the Irish catholics from their church facing the Common and the Jews. But best of all was the Fourth of July celebration, the bonfire lit the midnight before that blazed like the fire of Doom all night long and smoked all the next day, and the hours' long parade, the biggest in all the state and famous across the country, with the governor and politicians riding in it and white-haired veterans toddling behind and thousands of visitors from all over lining the streets, and the clapping and cheering for the old vets and war outfits and friends and relatives and notables going by.

Across the Common after several long blocks, Wood Street—at Collins, where Brand's was—sloped considerably on its way to The Ferry. Past Brand's, you passed the cove that opened onto the harbor and then the bay and then the Atlantic. All my life then was the water. Going down Wood to Brand's was a trip past the different streets my family had moved to, the houses we'd lived in before we settled on Hope near Bristol High the year before I entered.

Approaching the Stockmanns' big two-story frame house with the wide steps and long porch, where I'd spent so much time, I desired the meeting and dreaded it—desired home, his grandparents, but feared Brand, who would be everywhere in that house. Impossible to imagine it without him. Something in me didn't want to go back. Going back's too easy. But when I rang the bell the door opened almost immediately—they must have heard footsteps on the porch—and Mr. Stockmann for a second stared and then smiled, almost laughed, and cried, "Ferris!" He took my hand, drew me into the same quick scent of ripe apples and baking, into *then*. I was suddenly happily dislocated. Still holding my hand as the other slipped around my shoulder, he called, "Hertha, it's Ferris." She was there at the end of the corridor with a look of startled wonder, wiping her hands on the eternal apron as she came to me, appraising me for the least interval before she raised them—I might have been her Paul himself—and said, "Ferris, you."

I'd always seen them with the eyes of youth. How feeble and dried they were! They moved with the slow drift and dignity of ghosts, but in a minute they were not ghosts. Mrs. Stockmann, I saw, was almost breaking, but her embrace broke the spell. When she held me out, really taking me in, she smiled with such sweet joy. "*Du bist nach Hause gekommen. Gut! Komm.*" It struck me that secretly Brand must have clung to the sound of that language, their accent in English, and those often formal and complex sentences. She drew me by the hand to that kitchen, the nest of those old years, the talk place, the place of treats. With the three of us at the table, I felt like the prodigal, but there was no brother in that empty chair.

And at tea and toast with her plum preserves, it was a long slow morning. We meandered through Madrid and travels and the neighborhood deeps, gradually, as we grew closer to the reason for my coming, backtracking, meandering more and more as if we were following an exhausted stream that led to a spot we did not really want to reach, till at last we sat still in the sun falling over us and making the kitchen so bald—the high ceiling, the comfortable delft blue wallpaper, the cuckoo clock and temperature gauge with its woodman and his wife, a dish-towel embroidered *Bingen am Rhein*, the plaque reading *Gott, behüte dies Haus.*

Mr. Stockmann said, "You will need to go to his room."

She nodded. Her eye shifted, forlorn. "*Jetzt. Geh,*" she said, turning to her sink. "We have touched nothing. It is the same." She stood looking out on the posts and clothesline, the old stone well, and the green glider in the backyard.

"Always," his grandfather said, "Paul said he wanted you to have his things here, but that is written too in the will that he decided to make after Dean's death so Rich would have some financial help perhaps at a time when he needed it."

He accompanied me through the front hall to the stairway.

"You know the way," he said, wistful it seemed, and his voice faltered. "You will want to be alone."

Goya, Are You With Me Now?

I stared at the door until his steps ceased. From the kitchen I could hear only the muted murmur of their voices in those firm lickety-split German rhythms I relish so, ironically bringing Brand closer, who would not indulge in Huntsville. And I thought, Only they must know that speaking German here had been as comfortable as a soft blanket to Brand. He could let go here.

Then I opened the door, overwhelmed by sudden sun—and the view straight beyond. It was a fall day of infinite clarity and far over the houses and sloping land I could see the ridge of Mount Hope; and such a host of memories came (*Images, Ferris,* I heard Brand say then) of our treks through the woods of firs and sycamores and hemlock and maples and elms and oh the birches we'd made model Indian canoes from, hunting and hoarding arrowheads and artifacts, tracing history by following the Narragansetts and King Philip's trail to his stone seat on the mount beside his spring, where we'd drink, sometimes pitching a tent by the great outcrop of rocks overlooking the bay and Tiverton on the opposite shore, or lying warm in deep beds of pine needles under the thick trees in winter and seeking rest on ground cool as caves from the dew and rife green and damp in summer. In spring, toads tiny as fingernails hopped everywhere and rich moths blended with bark. We'd descend from the mount through the woods to the meadow two blocks below Brand's house, where a brook crossed between bald outcrops of stone interspersed with countless patches of blue forget-me-nots and the marsh where hundreds of deep purple iris quivered, and in the still waters we'd watch pollywogs, some already losing their tails and sprouting legs, turning frog. Across the road where the brook flowed fresh water toward the cove, armed with flashlights and spears we'd go night-fishing or in winter ice-fishing for eels. And in summer we'd avoid the kids in the cove and swim at the foot of Union Street, or Burton, where the great cup defenders against England, the yachts *Ranger I* and *II* and *Endeavor I* and *II* and others stood in drydock, the harbor filled with boats, always a regatta from the yacht club with blue, yellow, green, white, red sails billowed out by the wind streaking them over the water. Or we'd go diving off the pilings of the government dock into deep water, indifferent to floating oil wriggling like snakes on the surface and to the harmless sand sharks; or bike to The Ferry and over the bridge and make the run to the Moss's summer cottage at Island Park and swim with our friend Edith or row out to Gould Island.

Then I was staring at myself in the high bureau mirror between the two windows opposite the bedroom door, startled not to be that boy now. The room was all sun and silence, so deceptively the same that I might have been seventeen, waiting for Brand to come up to go on with our homework. Right of me, I saw in the mirror, were two enormous filing cabinets piled high too; and left, the almost ceiling-high bookcase his grandfather had surprised him with the year after he'd come from Huntsville—sixteen he was—and it too was jammed, but neat. Brand lived by order. There were the great brass double bed with a high bedside table and the big old-fashioned wrought-iron lamp to read by in bed. Several folded newspapers lay on it, unread perhaps. The worn paired armchairs, upholstered in a repeated tapestry of birds in a garden, were still neatly set on either end of the old Persian rug, facing the bed, their backs to Mount Hope. The floor—wide old pine boards—shone with midday sun; his grandmother had kept the room clean, though otherwise untouched. But what made it not the boy Brand's room, but the man's—what kept me in the present—was the raft of photos tacked to the walls, his choice shots no doubt. I recognized many, too many—history overwhelmed—and I realized how much time had passed since I had been in this room after high school graduation—thirty years!

I sat in the near chair for a long time before I touched anything. I sat staring at shots of war and rock concerts and starvation and protests and corruption and elections, the fruits of his years. It was only when I stirred and dared to face the desk that I could not avoid the boy—my friend, companion, right arm.

Between the two windows facing the backyard, his desk with

the two deep drawers on either side was piled high with papers. The bridge covered the wall. The bridge in fog. His earliest photos. *Images. I have lots of images. It makes you see what's really there.* And directly over the desk were Clara and Emily and Bett and I, and the class of '63, all pristine and ready for tomorrow.

Left, by the lamp, stood the framed photo I'd taken of my dog, Tommy.

I want you to have it, Brand.

Then I began. I opened the first drawer. There were the three years of exams, early notes on photography, projects, clippings about the class and photos, and letters to Huntsville from the girls, from me, and letters from Huntsville, mostly from his mother, a few from his father, and packets of Esther's, and Sylvia's, and finally the boys', and then a drawerful of letters from me, years of them, all arranged in that relentless order exacted in everything by his father. With each letter he was growing—through all the changes, the rigid boy, relaxed then, sometimes even spontaneously swaggering, the serious and responsible social-minded critic, the confused student of man's nature, the self tortured to doom and near extinction.

Hours I read—through puppy love and painful separations; cautions and admonitions from his father *to maintain always the highest standards, for only the finest work will put you where you belong;* praise from his mother *knowing what you can do, but, my dear son, do not overdo, be careful of your health* and her note *Do not be too hard on your father,* and his rush of memories to me of our foursome at my parents' place on Long Island, of meetings in Madrid, Paris, Verona, Amsterdam, Rome, his excitement at being a father, *to realize this strange responsibility makes me feel half helpless. I don't have Esther's confidence, but now I understand my bachelor freedom and you who have no children, though I prefer this responsibility—something in me has escaped into Dean and that's a new kind of freedom.* And interspersed in his war letters and increasingly in his jottings of his travels were comments and long passages on art, his quest in museums, churches, public buildings for the masterpieces. But the most illuminating notes were on Goya. How I remembered his face, stunned (what else can I say but *stunned*) by the Goyas, stunned *ecstatic* like the faces in paintings of saints transported by the sight of Jesus or the Virgin, a look like that; though more and more as the years passed came his other look, *blunted* then, a look of bewilderment before Goya's glorious achievements and the infinite possibilities of art and its challenge to transcend its very limits by channeling every impulse. He could no longer shake that look when he talked photography and what he saw and groped after; when he talked camera, limits, walls to climb—

How, Ferris?

I read into dusk, until I heard the quiet knock at his bedroom door.

"Ferris?"

I was too abruptly back in *now*.

"Come in."

"Forgive me. You are overdoing? Hungry you must be. You eat with us. Come, Papa is waiting."

Nights it was difficult to return to the immediate world of town and my mother's house. But each day I was easily lost to Wood Street—to Brand and his grandparents and lunch and afternoon tea with them and part of the evening back in his room. I was at home with their warm smiles, the eyes that fed on me, the voices so comfortable with a third at their table or upstairs in his room. I half expected them to call "Paul, dinner is ready. Paul, come down. Paul . . ."

Once I closed the door to Brand's room, I went out of time, down my life, ours. I felt I was walking into those photos, seeing with Brand's eyes what he had seen in those captured moments of the sixties and seventies and eighties. In the long run, in seeking to find images that actually capture a sense of the unceasing motion in things, what he had caught in major events was the flow of history.

He had a deep affinity with few of his photos.

"He had the habit," his grandmother told me, "of setting

one photo out in his study for weeks, and always in the same place there on the bookshelf as if he wanted to study it."

"The way you do a painting?" I suggested.

"Exactly!" she said.

"Then he'd take it down and never put that one up again. There was one," she said, "my favorite, of that Bob Dylan at Woodstock." *Voodstuk.* Her accent almost made me turn to see if Brand were behind me. "But he was crazy for one of his first, of the—folk singer you say here too, not?—Joan Baez in California."

You should see my Baez.

My Baez. I could hear that now. Because it *was* his. He had loved that photo. He had had his reasons. It was among his things, one of his personal, intimate, even secret treasures, one of those rarities he'd hardly discuss with me. There *were* those photos that he did not discuss with anyone, even me. And I always knew they were important to him precisely because he refused to comment on them—no, not refused to comment, but simply remained silent—and I came to know that he remained silent precisely to communicate something he could not say: it was his way of making me perceive something important; it was his intuitive way of sharing with me, because though he had words, though he could write well, before some aspects of his vision he could not articulate. Besides, the photograph articulated; and if it did not, he could not have gone further, he had captured all he had seen at that moment and the photograph had to speak for itself since it was his essential way of speaking. For him there was no other way of speaking about *what he saw.* And it was that wall of silence, when I met it in him, which was his way of alerting me. I knew his intentions. And he expected me to know his intentions. He would have been appalled if I hadn't realized he was depending on me to see how far he'd gone and how far he'd fallen short—because it was his desperation always that he had fallen short, as if his desperation itself had to be fed with failure to maintain his desperation, as if desperation were the very means to make him go on to seek more intensively what it was that was still missing, though a photograph might seem a masterpiece to the press, public, his friends and fellow professionals. Oh, yes, he *could* talk. And he would. He would talk hours about technique. "But what after all is technique but *the midwife?*" he'd say.

Yes, I remembered the photo. The Baez was a marvel. It is a moment of uncanny true magic. It exposes all fake faith. Baez is singing. Baez is sitting with her guitar and singing. She is some distance from the camera. She is on a height. She is in the middle of a circle. She is surrounded by people sitting, thousands and thousands of people with their heads raised, listening to her sing. The heads and all those bodies surround her in an arena of living flesh. Does she gather them all together? Do they gather her to them? Neither one nor the other. Both? Though she is sitting on a height in the middle of them, so extensive is the endless circle of heads in the photograph that she appears also to be sunk in the middle of them. She has such simplicity and virginal beauty that you might even expect a halo, and there is a halo, but the halo is not over her head, the innumerable concentric circles of heads are the halo, she is part of the halo, there is one halo, and the halo is alive, and the halo is all flesh.

I felt I knew now what Brand had captured in the photo, *what had happened to him*, what it was: He heard the singer. He heard the song. He heard the *singing*. The singing binds them together. They *are* the singing. He wanted to capture the true singing. To him the photograph had captured the singing. The photograph is silent, and the silence is filled. The silence is singing.

Of course the singing was not there. What I was hearing was his voice in his letters.

Mornings at dawn or before, I took long vigorous walks as I do in Madrid. I was never one to sleep late, and under the impetus of Brand, hungry to gather and hoard against time what I once took for granted, I wouldn't waste the days. I had to see the town. Though my roots were here, I'd become a stranger to it, yet Brand had kept it his. I felt I was seeing it for the last time, though I knew the thought was absurd, for as long as my mother, Esther, and Rich, and of course the Stockmanns were still in Bristol, I would return, if not so often. Madrid was my place now. But Brand had stirred silt, and I set out each morning to a different section of town—first the harbor, past Guiteras Junior High, then Mill Pond, along the road winding around the harbor to Poppasquash Point; then along the Neck toward Warren, past where "the poor house" had once been—we'd climb the stone wall and crawl to the windows and stare in and try to get the looneys' attention and then scoot scared as hell when we did; then to the forbidden territory of *wops* and *portygees*, over to the Kickemuit River narrows; and then to the U.S. Rubber Company and the three-story tenement houses that seemed to gather around the gigantic brick smokestack you could see for blocks around and feel tremble the ground when it hooted out twelve and five o-clock; then the length of Metacom Avenue that cut through almost all the town "classes"; and the old heart of town, once Anglo-Saxon but now, my mother said, almost all bought up by Italian and Portuguese, who ran the town.

I didn't realize until later how unconsciously I was systematically laying out the town, how Brand's calling me back had led me to the years before that day he had appeared in Miss Bradford's English class. And on the fourth morning it startled that I found myself standing before a strange house on Woodlawn Avenue in no way resembling the green and white cottage I had been born in on that very spot, so startled me that I had then to go back just the two blocks to Brand's grandparents' house on the corner of Wood and Collins to verify where I was, and who. How, I thought, do those two old people, uprooted to a second life forty-eight years before, cut off from their world, blood, and language in a town not actively hostile but not actively hospitable, with the heart of their lives gutted, and with Rich mostly out of sight . . ., how did they know who they were?

Exiles.

Each of us.

All.

Brand.

He was agitated by his life during his early years in Huntsville. He was born with the Rocket Team, grew up with it, every day surrounded by experiments, their failures and successes, and with their stress on *out there*. No wonder his natural impulse was doubly driven and his vision was always fixed on some image that contained the promise, the impossible answers to the impossible question:

"What are we, Ferris?"

Exiles in the universe, making our way—valiantly, like his exiled grandparents and hosts of others—into greater exile and calling each place home, knowing reason is not strong enough to stop what's in us that yearns, dreams, reaches up, out—

Years after he had left Huntsville—in our meetings in this city or that, at home or abroad, at his studio or his parents' or grandparents' house—sooner or later whenever we were viewing his photos, there would come that stare long and hard, as if his vision, so clear to him a moment before, were subtly blunted by the hard objects that he could not see *through*, as if his hand itself, reaching out to touch whatever lived in his vision, struck a hard thing and the imagined sight vanished. He would look up at me then, more curious than pained, as if to ask *What are we doing here?* And I was sure that he was silently asking himself again that other question, *What are we?*, which devastated when you thought about it.

I ask those questions now, I asked them in his room, hearing the far sounds of his grandparents in the rooms below—steps, voices, doors—and seeing not this September day outside but the spring days of then: in the yard the forsythia, a still fountain of yellow, and daffodils, and the lilac buds. *April is the cruelest month*. It splits the earth but yields such beauty. And I could hear us kids in school singing about April showers that bring May flowers.

May flowers.

What I was seeing then was the flower stuck in the barrel of a gun at the Kent State uprising. Across twenty-three years came the flower, and Brand's voice. And it was the appalling sound in his voice at the mystery of the impulse in us that so had fascinated him to excitement and then to numbness because it roused us to violence and freedom, the one worth the other.

There were his photos of the 1970 student rebellion.

In May he flew to Ohio. Kent State students had held an anti-war rally, stoned the ROTC building, marched toward the president's house, burned the Constitution. The National Guard was sent out, six hundred. Tear gas. Fires. Twelve students arrested. And on a second day another injured and fifteen arrested. And on a third, four students shot and eight wounded in the breakup of a thousand students rallying on the campus commons— because of a shot outside the National Guard, the Guard would maintain. And who knew? But because *fear*.

"The students were afraid, Ferris—afraid, and not. And brave from fear too. And the Guards were cowards from fear, and human from fear, but had to protect the love and fear because love and fear are always waiting in us whenever people are together, aren't they? Something in us—the same thing?— binds us and separates us—since the beginning—since animals —we *are*—every *single* minute killing from fear and love some-where, in Sri Lanka Beijing Dublin San Salvador California Morocco Haiti. The motion never stops. It's always seeking our weak spot to erupt from— Is that it? It moves forever. It's as wild as all nature in spring, all the nightmares of May."

He could not escape Goya.

"My God, Ferris, you'd think Goya's paintings of the shoot-ings of May had come to life. And on the same days! May 2 and 3 and 4! You'd think it was two centuries ago in Goya's day. Reaping justice, reaping horror. I keep seeing Goya: the horror on the face of that Spanish victim about to be shot by Napo-leon's grenadiers, his arms flung to the sky in a cross, and the shock of his stark white shirt beside the stark blood on the dead civilians lying at his feet, pure white and pure red. But what is it? Goya didn't know. But he painted it. And the Russian poet

Yevtushenko painted it in his poem to the student Krause killed by the National Guard: she puts a flower in the muzzle of the guard's gun."

Here in his room he couldn't escape the May shootings. I couldn't now. Hanging there were Brand's photos of Kent State and small reproductions of Goya's paintings of the second and third of May 1808, the chaotic clash between Spaniards and Mamelukes and the shooting down the file of helpless civilians on Principe Pío mount in Madrid. And Brand had slides of all Goya's black paintings, his monsters.

"Surely the students had all the revolutions of May in mind. My Kent State photos are merely one more in the cycle."

"Cycle?"

"Of madness. It's natural to erupt, but people fabricate their own sun and seethe and break out. Don't you see, Ferris? Something in our body wants to leave us; it has to break out, even *more* in spring when everything's pressing to erupt. Madness will out, it seems, and not only in revolutions. Look at Goya's pilgrims—hordes of monsters deformed and sick and deranged, despairing of all reason, letting madness out by banding together on a pilgrimage to San Isidro to seek a miracle. The canvas is black but for the faces and distant light. The light reveals the mad faces. If light's part of madness, how can you hold it back?"

"You have to let it out in the right way, at the right time."

"The right way! The right time! You have to recognize what madness is. And we don't—until after—and even then . . . Reason's tricky. It's just part of what impels us. Reason can turn to madness too, the worst kind."

It was no *idea* to Brand. It was too real. It was his greatest cause for despair.

"I've followed it all over the world. I didn't have to, God knows. It was right in my—" He caught the word. "Look at how *he* erupted because of Esther's Jewish blood and what he did. No, nobody has to go far—it's in us. We were taught there will be wars and rumors of wars in Sunday school and home, weren't we? before we ever knew war. But kids don't have to be taught. We shot, stabbed, and battered each other, and over what?—marbles and comic books, home runs and bikes and baseball cards."

When I'd gone through the papers in the last of the desk drawers, I heard a thud like the sound of a creature landing. I reached in. My hand met a small book. I had seen it once before. He had kept it standing upright behind those papers—hidden. It was his father's German copy of that little book by a Pole—"but an aristocratic Pole," his father had told Brand. His father's full name, *Heinrich Paul Brand*, was written on the flyleaf. I flicked through it to those terrible words I had accidentally come upon years before. Yes, there the phrase was, boldly underlined in ink—browned now, but obviously red once: *Rottet alle die Viecher aus.*

Holding that book and seeing those words made me tremble. *Exterminate all the brutes.*

Why had Brand kept it? Was it the only intimate thing he'd had of his father's? the most revealing? the one concrete evidence of his father's destructive nature? Had he kept it so as never to forget? to torture himself with his father's nature and his fear of his own? Or couldn't he part with the most terrible secret? Maybe he treasured it out of that perversity that sometimes holds us against our will because we feel an undeniable kinship with it. He must have believed that perversity bound him forever to his father? There was no escape.

And none for me now.

It was late Friday morning. I had been over two weeks a good part of the time in his room, and now, that bittersweet task ended, a feeling of melancholy overcame me at the sudden emptiness. With nothing more to do I felt forced to admit with the last paper an end to his physical existence. Brand was gone —I didn't deceive myself—yet he was closer to me. Going through his papers I had lived an experience he could only have denied me when alive, and which had led me back as far as memory could reach into my own childhood—the house that was gone now, the brook the kids used to shove me into and run, my baby rabbits washed up under the shed in a flood, the meadow and Tanyard Lane, the cove and harbor that had been my life. And the journey had brought my people back to life for an interval. Every day I had sat long with those memories. I could have sat hours then too, lost, but I had to go down to tell his grandparents I had finished at last. I dreaded telling them, I dreaded *not* coming day after day, I dreaded the look that would come over their faces when time came to say good-bye.

"I'm through," I said.

"Not," his grandmother said.

"There's more," his grandfather said.

"*Im Keller*," she said.

"The cellar!"

"Yes," his grandfather said. "In the rec room."

He meant the room behind the furnace.

"He had there his studio," she said.

"Studio?"

"*Ja*. Nobody to enter. It was *verboten*."

Forbidden.

"But not to you," I said.

"No, no. But why would we enter when it was his? He kept it locked, but always here was the key." He handed me a key hung from a nail on the kitchen door frame.

"But haven't you been down?" I asked it of both of them.

"Yes," he said. "There is the letter."

"For you." She turned away. "Where he left it," she said.

The door to the cellar stairs was midway in the passageway between the back entry hall and the living room. The steps descended to the wide area the length of the house, where she hung laundry to dry in bad weather and which Brand and I had used when we weren't in his room.

The right half of the cellar was partitioned off and that too was divided in half, the front half the furnace room with the coal bin and the back half the rec room. Between the two was a narrow alleyway with a door to each and latticework for dividers. Actually the partitions were flimsy and anyone could peer through the slats. I stood in the half-light a moment. I heard footsteps above, but not voices.

The padlock popped open and I latched it in the hasp.

Since the rec room extended under the kitchen ell, bricked against an earth wall, there was no back window, the only daylight coming from the overhead side window. I skirted a long dark stretch of table and swept my arm out for the bulb that hung somewhere midway, if I remembered right, and struck the cord and jerked it.

I felt I'd lose my breath.

The room was filled with faces.

Paintings.

Even in that dim light faces stared from the shadows. The dark was filled with them, they lined the walls, they were set on the floor. A face stared at me from the easel, and two from easels set back, enormous heads.

I was breathing hard. I stood there a long time, taking in those faces and the stack of canvases against the rear wall. Beside me was a long table with pots, trays, tins, brushes, palette cups, and knives. The floor under it and beyond was littered with cans, supplies—no order here, all chaos.

Brand!

I moved when I saw the photographer's lamp on the left. He had run an extension cord through the slats. I connected the lamp.

Light flooded like day.

It destroyed the faces. I stared at the face on the center easel. But it was not a face. It was a head, but not a head. When I went close, the head had no true outline, no lineaments. I examined the others all about the room. They were all heads, but the effect was the same—of magnified motes, particles, dissolution. Close, the form was lost. The canvas was white, light, and what made the suggestion of a head were dabs, smears, streaks of paint, oils, each absolutely isolated. What would be eyes, nose, mouth was space. Dabs and brush strokes surrounded them. They were mere spaces. There was no real form. Myriad black markings blocked out white space in some attempt to shape over or accentuate it. I scrutinized it—there were what looked like holes in the black dabs and smears and strokes; white broke through everywhere. Black blighted the light, and light blighted the black.

When I backed off, they were vague semblances of faces again.

A man's.

But whose?

I went over them again and again for the least characteristic to identify who they might be. At times I thought merely from some vaguely overall shape of the heads—longer, narrower, wide, round—his father, that boy, Rich, Dean. Actually they were too basically the one thing, a head in the process of decomposition, most of them long and narrow, though from the composition I was certain that he was trying to create form out of dissolution, trying to capture the motion of matter and what was always happening in the spaces.

But he had failed—again.

They were chaotic images of light and dark, separate and inseparable.

I knew too well what he'd been after in his photos.

He wanted to paint what was in that boy, in everybody.

He wanted to paint what was in his father.

He could only destroy his father. He *wanted* to destroy his father. And he wanted to *recreate* him.

But what was in his father defied the form Brand *wanted to give it.*

Brand couldn't lie. He could only repeat that head, endlessly. He could see only the man his father was—there was no other. One thing he *did* achieve: as *he* struggled, he painted out the chaos of dark and light seething in inexplicable combination.

The vision must have come from whatever his father had done, whatever Brand believed or imagined or knew his father had been responsible for.

He couldn't escape the father in him.

He couldn't recreate him—he *could* not—so he had to destroy what was in him.

In how many ways—and how many times—had he tried to kill his father?

Was that it, Brand?

He wanted—I could hear him, I hear him now—he wanted images that penetrated the visible and arrested the motion of matter . . .

". . . if only you could make the camera lens your eye and go into the photo so deep you could enter the spaces between the most infinite particles and know the silent music, the form of the music, go so far into the silence that your body dissolves into the matter of space and the space of matter. Sometimes when staring at a painting I feel I become the substance of the space that is in the paint and the space that is not the paint. The secret is the texture. That's what makes the difference in effect between *still life* and *arrested motion*. Arrested motion convinces you that time and motion actually exist in the painting. Yes, texture is the secret. You're in a split second of life. Time is moving. You could walk into it and be at home. But a photo affirms only memory and time gone."

But he couldn't capture time moving. In photography that was impossible.

So in secret he had turned to painting. He had holed himself up here in the basement and painted himself out.

And how he had guarded his secret!

I stared at the head on the easel. Brand had stopped midway in the painting. He couldn't finish it. He had abandoned it, defeated.

His father had had control of his own passion. He had made a vile art of it—annihilation. But Brand could *not* capture that passion; he couldn't make art of his passion and triumph over his father's destructive impulse. And if he couldn't, he could choose, he chose— Did you, Brand? Was that it?—to control his own life and turn that terrible image of annihilation back on his father.

157

I lined the canvases along the walls. I felt surrounded. I went over canvas after canvas. I stared at them I don't know how long.

I can't recreate—I don't want to—the sensations I experienced then; but I was dead cold and I had the hopeless feeling of falling apart and wondering *how to get hold*.

Sounds brought me back—footsteps, the back door opening and closing, steps on the porch, the door again, and a voice, his grandfather's, then hers—those sounds that are the everyday music that saves most of us from the threat of that farther music. Those voices roused me from my bewilderment, though it was some time before I could go up and face his grandparents.

I disconnected the lamp and jerked the cord to the bulb. When I turned to leave, in the half-light I saw the white envelope. It was tacked to the left frame of the door so I couldn't miss it on the way out.

My name was written in bold letters.

It was sealed.

"Brand . . .," I said.

He came too much to life.

I was afraid to open it.

It held a torn sliver of paper smeared with black paint.

Burn everything.

Burn—!

I leaned against the wall.

Burn everything.

But why hadn't *he* burned it?

They were—surely they were—for his eyes only.

Since he'd written the note, he must have decided what he was going to do—he'd have to drive to Providence, go to the studio . . .

I imagined him sitting at his desk as Esther and then Rick had described him, his head wrapped in plastic, a faceless face . . .

Burn everything.

Burning them himself would have taken too much time. It would have announced his suicide.

Or he'd had no time. In a passion he'd written the note; in a passion he'd driven to the studio, fearing his impulse might have weakened . . .

No, that passion had possessed him for too many years. Too many years he'd warded it off. . . .

But the two weeks of that murder trial and the long period between the sentencing and the electrocution, which coincided with his collapse, or triggered it . . . *was* that the straw—? All that year—all his life—he'd been in limbo between innocence and guilt, and that trial and sentence he must have taken as his father's, brought out *for him* into public light.

If his father was on trial, he was.

We all were.

The jury had pronounced Galt guilty. Brand had judged himself—and sentenced himself:

And wanted his life effaced, all, as impossible as that was. He was famous, but failed. His photos were in archives everywhere. But who knew what he had dared? No one. No one would ever know.

But I knew.

Burn everything.

He'd left that for me to do.

Now I saw why he hadn't left all to Rich.

Above all, he wanted *me* to see the paintings. He wanted me to destroy him.

Why, Brand?

Standing there with the scrap in my hand, I thought all those thoughts at once, confused as if confronted by a nest of riled snakes. It seemed long—it wasn't—before I put the scrap back in the envelope and kept it in my shirt pocket, shut and padlocked the door—and went up to this grandparents.

After the cellar, the sight of day and things and his people was comforting.

His grandparents were waiting not so much with curiosity as with apprehension.

Perhaps they were measuring my reaction.

"You've seen his paintings?" I said.

They nodded.

"Horrible." She flattened her hands against her thighs and kept them there.

"How long had he been working down there?"

"Many months—every chance he had—since maybe . . ."

"Since?"

"A year, maybe more, last spring or so."

Since the trial.

I told them, "The note said burn everything."

They gazed flatly at me.

At last his grandfather said, "Burn the paintings?"

"Everything, he said."

A little sink sounded in her throat, but neither spoke. His grandfather's lashes flicked, and his head cocked upward, like listening.

Then she turned from us. "Some tea, Ferris—and bread and preserves." And busied herself. The table was already set. "Sit."

For a while she veered the talk. They were thinking of taking a trip at last to Germany, the first since the Hitler war—almost fifty years! "If we make it!" (They must have been ninety.) They had relatives they didn't know, born after the war, all they had left over there. They were excited, yes, but afraid. "We maybe won't recognize our place. We'll be strangers—in our land. But the land does not change, the mountains, no, and the rivers, and the old things. And you, you think you might make a trip to Germany then?"

"You could come to Madrid—and know Carmen."

"Ach, the cost," she said.

"Hertha," he said.

"Always I am too practical." She laughed. "But I stand so. And then there is the Spanish language, and my tongue would stumble." And laughed again.

"But you will always come here," his grandfather said.

"And with maybe Carmen. We would know her, if we could."

"You will one of these days."

We escaped into the future. But met silence. And returned. They waited. Brand's *everything* was mine now.

They might have been staring into his empty room or the empty cellar.

I couldn't tell what grief their stoic looks locked in, though I could guess how great a treasure merely the presence of Brand's possessions was to them. What they could touch.

I said, "And would you burn everything?" I looked at him. At her.

He didn't hesitate. "That is not a question to be asked."

"You're sure?"

"*Ja. Was du willst,*" he said, his language baring him.

"It is what he wanted," I said.

His grandmother nodded, her lids wet.

"I'll come in the morning," I said.

At home I went through tortuous doubts, my mother quickly aware because of my drifting off into unusual silences, but as always she didn't meddle, she knew I'd tell her—*when*, and if. It was blasphemy to destroy his papers and those paintings. It would be a betrayal of his vision. Who, then, would ever know what he had attempted? And if I did *not* burn everything, I'd betray Brand's trust, sacred trust—it *was*—because Brand never played false games. If *he'd* wanted to burn them, he'd have done it. If he hadn't wanted *me* to burn them, he'd not have been so determined. If I did burn them, wouldn't I be betraying whoever *out there* might benefit by them? If I didn't, wouldn't I betray *me*, who considered his friendship sacred, who was the only person alive—and Brand had known that—who understood his world, even his impossible world. In destroying part of his world, wasn't I destroying part of my own?

All this, of course, was the aftermath, self-recrimination for a decision I wouldn't—couldn't—change.

In the morning I went back—and all that day and the next I carried boxes of papers down to the furnace and burned them. Last, I cut the canvases from the wood braces and one after the other thrust them into the fire. In an instant of remorse I was tempted to hold one back, belie everything. *One*, Brand. I'd have given anything if something in the canvases had defied fire and preserved them as untouched as Shadrach, Mashach, and Abednego in the fiery furnace. The flame gave those faces such sudden life that I could have thrust my hand into the flame to save them—then they leaped, turned monstrous, and collapsed and dissolved to nothing.

Before going, I threw all his supplies into the trash and swept the rec room. Only the lamp and easels remained.

Then I went back up to his room. I closed the door. I sat at the empty desk.

The room took on the long September shadows. Outside, the trees lay long shadows, and the houses, and only the ridge of Mount Hope caught light, thinning fast as the minutes went.

The room slowly sank in the dusk.

I didn't put on the light.

When I finally moved, I put the little framed photo of my dog, Tommy, in my jacket pocket—it was, after all, the only thing really mine—and went down and said good-bye to his grandparents.

When I called Carmen, she said, "It's bad?"

"Bad enough. I'll tell you."

"Pain's part of grief."

"What do Spaniards do when they suffer?"

"They sing," she said.

I laughed.

"You'll know one day what he did for you."

"Did for me?"

"Because he knew you too."

"You mystify me."

"And Brand did."

"Some."

"Then you'll have to penetrate the mystery—both mysteries."

She laughed softly, but I knew how serious the edge of her casual laughter could be.

The last morning in Bristol, true to late September, the

harbor was obscured by fog. Hog Island and Prudence, and Poppasquash Point across the harbor, were not visible. I took the long trek down Hope, through downtown, along the waterfront, past where the cove rounded into Wood Street straight to The Ferry. I stood at the foot of the bridge. In the fog the great girders stood half visible, skeletal bones made gray by the gray air, the bridge arching into the deep fog, the cables in long graceful sweep over the dark waters of the bay, the bridge itself vanishing into the white deeps the sun would burn off later on.

I stood at the foot of the bridge a long time staring into the fog. I felt I was standing inside one of Brand's photographs and unless I found the way I would never get out.